MY WORN-OUT SANDAL clipped a vine, and I nearly fell over. Massa construction workers looked up and stared at me weirdly. Did they know? Maybe the good news had been sent out to them over some kind of Massaweb. What were they thinking?

All hail, King Jack!

His Royal Highness, Jack the First of Belleville!

A good day to His Jackness, Master of the Kingdom of Atlantis and Ruler of the World!

Sooner or later everyone was going to have to adjust to King Jack. Including me.

The Tides Turn

SEVEN
WONDERS

THE
CURSE
OF THE
KING

PETER LERANGIS

HARPER

An Imprint of HarperCollinsPublishers

Seven Wonders Book 4: The Curse of the King
Text by Peter Lerangis, copyright © 2014 by HarperCollins Publishers
Illustrations copyright © 2014 by Torstein Norstrand
Map art by Mike Reagan, copyright © 2014 by HarperCollins Publishers

Library of Congress Control Number: 2015288095
ISBN 978-0-06-207050-0

Design by Joe Merkel
16 17 18 19 20   CG/OPM   10 9 8 7 6 5 4 3 2 1
❖
First paperback edition, 2016

FOR MOM AND DAD,
WHO HAVE READ EVERYTHING
SINCE THE VERY FIRST SENTENCE

TIGRIS

EUPHRATES

THE · HANGING · GARDENS
OF · BABYLON

RUSALEM

PERSIAN · GULF

SEA

M I L E S

0   100   200   300   400   500

CHAPTER ONE
THE WRATH OF YAPPY

HAVING LESS THAN a year to live doesn't feel great, but it's worse when you're in a cop car that smells of armpits, cigarettes, and dog poop. "Don't New York City cops ever clean their cars?" Cass Williams mumbled.

I turned my nose to the half-open window. Aly Black was at the other end of the backseat, but Cass was stuck in the middle. Outside, music blared from a nearby apartment window. An old woman walking a Chihuahua eyed us and began yelling something I couldn't quite make out.

"Okay, what do we do now, Destroyer?" Cass asked.

"'Jack' is still my name," I said.

"'The Destroyer Shall Rule,' that was the prophecy," Aly replied. "And your mom pointed at you."

"We were invisible! She could have been pointing at . . ." My voice trailed off. It was after midnight, but the way they were both glaring at me, I felt like I needed sunglasses. I was beginning to think throwing that last Loculus under a train might not have been a great idea. "Look, I'm sorry. I really am. But I had to do it, or everyone would have died. You would have done the same thing!"

Aly sighed. "Yeah, you're right. It's just . . . an adjustment, that's all. I mean, we had a chance. And now . . ."

She gave me a sad shrug. *We're dead*, is what she didn't say. A genetic mutation was on target to kill us before the age of fourteen. And I had sabotaged our chance to be cured. Seven Loculi was what we needed. Now one of them was in pieces under a train.

I sank back into the smelly seat. As the car slowed to a stop in front of a squat brick police station, our driver called out, "Home sweet home!"

She was a tall, long-faced woman named Officer Wendel. Her partner, Officer Gomez, quickly hauled himself out from the passenger side. He was barely taller than me but twice my width. The car rose an inch or so when he exited. "Your papa's inside, dude," he said. "Make nice with him and make sure we don't see you again."

"You won't," Aly replied.

"Wait!" cried the old woman with the Chihuahua. *"Those are devil children!"*

Officer Gomez paused, but another cop waved him in. "You go ahead," he said wearily. "We'll take care of Mrs. Pimm."

"I recognize her," Aly whispered. "She's the person who shows up in movie credits as Crazy New York City Neighbor."

As Officer Gomez rushed us inside and down a short, grimy hallway, I eyed my backpack, which was slung over his shoulder. The Loculus of Flight and the Loculus of Invisibility formed two big, round bulges.

He had peeked inside but not too carefully. Which was lucky for us.

Officer Wendel walked ahead and pushed open the door to a waiting room. Dad was sitting on a plastic chair, and he stood slowly. His face was drawn and pale.

"Officers Gomez and Wendel, Washington Heights Precinct," Gomez said. "We responded to the missing-persons alert. Found them while investigating a commotion up by Grant's Tomb."

"Thank you, officers," Dad said. "What kind of commotion? Are they in trouble?"

"Healthy and unharmed." Gomez unhooked the pack and set it on a table. "We had reports of noises, people in costume—gone by the time we got there."

Officer Wendel chuckled. "Well, a few weirdoes in robes near the train tracks, picking up garbage. Guess the party was over. Welcome to New York!"

Dad nodded. "That's a relief. I—I'll take them home now."

He reached for the backpack, but Officer Wendel was already unzipping it and looking inside. "Just a quick examination," she said with an apologetic look. "Routine."

"Officer Gomez did it already!" I pointed out.

Before Gomez could respond, a sharp barking noise came from the hallway. The old lady was inside, with her dog. Officer Wendel looked toward the noise.

I reached for the pack, but Wendel pulled it away. She opened my canvas sack and removed the basketball-sized Loculus of Flight. "Nice . . ." she said.

"A world globe," I blurted. "We have to . . . paint the countries onto—"

"What the . . . ?" Officer Wendel's hand had hit the invisible second Loculus.

"It's nothing!" Cass blurted out.

"Literally," Aly added.

Wendel tried to wriggle the Loculus out. "Is this glass?"

"A special kind of glass," Dad said. "So clear I'll bet you can't see it!"

"Wow . . ." Wendel said. She lifted her hands high, holding up . . . absolutely nothing. Nothing that the human eye could see, that is. "I can feel it, but I can't—"

"*I am not crazy stop treating me like I'm crazy, I saw them, I tell you—they were floating like birds!*" Mrs. Pimm's voice was rising to a shriek—and I remembered where I'd heard

4

her voice and seen her face.

An open window, a dim light. She had been staring at us as the Shadows from the Mausoleum at Halicarnassus lifted us through the streets. She'd been one of the only people who'd noticed the flurries of darkness, the fact that we were being borne down the street in the invisible arms of Artemisia's minions.

I darted toward the door and looked out.

Yiiiii! The Chihuahua saw me first. He wriggled out of her arms and skittered down the hallway toward me, baring his teeth.

"There—those are the wicked children!" Now Mrs. Pimm was heading our way, followed by two burly cops. "They were floating above the ground . . . talking to spirits! *Come back here, Yappy!*"

I sprang back into the room as Yappy clattered inside, yapping away.

Officer Wendel let go of the backpack. She and Gomez surrounded Yappy, reaching for his collar. Mrs. Pimm began lashing at them with her cane. Two other cops grabbed at her shoulders.

"Where's the Loculus?" Aly whispered.

There.

I couldn't see it, but I saw a perfectly rounded indentation in the sack on the table—a logical place where an invisible sphere might be resting. Shoving my hand toward the air above it, I felt a cool, round surface.

Now I could see the Loculus. Which meant I was invisible. "Got it!"

Aly sidled close to me. I reached out and grabbed her hand. Just before she disappeared, Cass reached for her, too.

Dad stood there against the wall, looking confused. Now Cass and Aly both had hands on the Loculus, so I let go of Aly and reached toward Dad with my free hand. "If you touch us," I said softly, "the power transfers."

He flinched when I took his arm. But it was nothing like the looks on the faces of Mrs. Pimm and the group of police officers. Their jaws were nearly scraping the floor. A cup of coffee lay in a puddle below them.

I could hear Yappy heading for the entrance as fast as his little legs could carry him.

We followed after him, but we didn't rush.

Even the NYPD can't stop something they can't see.

CHAPTER TWO

TWERP PERPS, SNALP, AND THE FAT LADY

DAD'S DISGUISE WAS a porkpie hat and a fake, glued-on mustache that made him sneeze. Aly's hair, colored blond with cheap spray-on hair color bought at Penn Station, was bunched into a baseball cap. Cass wore a hoodie and a fake scar on his cheek, and I opted for thick sunglasses, which were now hurting my nose.

Dad and Aly sat on one side of a narrow table, Cass and I on the other. We were the only ones in our little train compartment, which made our disguises kind of ridiculous. At least I thought so.

None of us had been able to sleep. Now the countryside was aglow with the first hints of the morning sun. "We are two hundred forty-nine miles into Pennsylvania, fifty-four point three miles from the Ohio border," Cass announced.

"Thank you, Mr. GPS," Aly said.

"Seriously, how can you do that?" I asked. "The angle of the sun?"

"No," Cass replied, gesturing out the window toward a narrow post that zoomed by. "The mile markers."

Dad covered his mouth. *"Ahh-haaaa-choo!"*

"Guys, maybe we can take off the disguises?" Aly said. "I've been checking news sites, feeds, social media, and there's nothing about us."

"What if we're America's Most Wanted?" Cass asked. "What if our pictures are in every post office from here to Paducah?"

Wincing, Dad pulled off his mustache. "Cass, let's examine that word—*wanted*. The best way to predict how people will act is knowing what they *want*. One thing the New York police don't want is the press to know that four people vanished from under their noses."

"'Tonight's headline: Twerp perps pop from cops! Details at eleven!'" Cass said.

Aly pulled back her newly blond hair into a scrunchie. "When we get to Chicago, I'm washing out this disgusting color."

"Your hair was *blue* before this," Cass remarked.

Aly stuck out her tongue.

"I think it looks nice," I said, quickly adding, "not that

blue wasn't nice. It was. So was the orange."

Aly just stared at me bewildered, like I'd just said something in Sanskrit. I turned away. Sometimes I should just keep my mouth shut.

Cass cracked up. "Maybe she can borrow the red coloring from your skin."

"Once we're in Chicago, Aly, you're getting on a plane to Los Angeles," Dad said. "To see your mom."

"What am I going to tell her?" Aly asked.

"The truth," Dad replied. "She has to know everything. And she has to keep what happened to you a secret—"

"She won't do that!" Aly said. "I mean—I vanished for weeks. She's going to open a federal investigation!"

Dad shook his head. "Not when she realizes what's at stake. That there's still a hope of curing you kids. Our job now is to create an airtight alibi, which we all will use. It has to explain why three kids disappeared and then slipped back weeks later, all at the same time. We have to somehow contain this. People in our hometown are going to ask questions. Yours, too, Aly."

"So . . . um . . ." Cass said uneasily. "How do I figure into these snalp?"

"Snalp?" Dad said.

"*Plans*," I translated. "It's Backwardish. Remember? He uses it when he's feeling silly. Or nervous."

"Or deracs," Cass added.

Dad looked him straight in the eyes. He knew about Cass's background. Honestly, I couldn't imagine what Cass was thinking. Mainly because I don't know what's it's like to have two parents in jail on a robbery conviction. What I did know was that he'd be sent back to child services until he was eighteen. Which meant, under our circumstances, forever.

"Of course I have plans," Dad said. "Don't you y-worr . . . wy-orr . . ."

"Yrrow?" Cass said. "As in, *worry*?"

Dad was already scribbling on a sheet of legal paper. "Exactly," he said.

"Okay then, I won't," Cass said, looking very, very worried.

* * *

"Next station stop, Chicago, Illinois!"

As the conductor's voice echoed in the train car, the sun burned through the window. Aly and Cass had fallen asleep, and I was almost there, too.

Dad's eyes were bloodshot as he put the final touches on the list we'd been working on for hours. I read it for about the hundredth time.

"Um," I said.

Aly sighed. "Complicated."

"Out of our minds," Cass added.

"I think we can make it work," Dad said with a deep breath.

1. Jack loses memory in B.ville hospital. Wanders off in middle of night.

Get corrob. From Dr. Flood. All true.

Rick S. will vouch. Lives in H'ville, works for med supplier to MGL, never met J.

2. J. ends up in woods in Hopperville, falls asleep. Found by anonymous homeless guy.

Email Walsh. He owes favor or 2.

Get applic. papers ASAP. ← – – –

3. Homeless guy contacts Rick S*, who can't ID Jack but recognizes he needs sophisticated treatment. Sends J. to Stanford, CA.

4. In Stanford, Dr. Walsh* brings back J.'s memory.

5. Walsh contacts Dad, who flies out to get J.

6. While in hospital, J. rooms with accident victim who is a hardened street tough but nice guy (Cass). They bond.

7. Upon meeting Cass, Dad decides to begin legal adoption.

NOTE: Call Aly's mom, work out alibi for her.
* College friends of Dad. Will work with us.

"I like the 'hardened street tough' part," Cass said.

"Now for your story, Aly," Dad went on. "We need something your mom can jump on board with."

"Mom and I are no strangers to alibis," Aly said. "I've been working with covert government groups for a long time. We can say I was on a CIA project. Much less complicated than your epic lie."

Dad removed his porkpie hat and ran his fingers through his steadily graying hair. "One thing you need to know, guys. Your disappearances have been in the news. Luckily for us, the reports have stayed local. Three separate communities, three separate disappearances, three different times. Well, four, including Marco. Now three of you are showing up at once. Up to now, no one has connected the disappearances. That's our task—containing the stories. Keeping them strictly local news."

"No publicity," Aly agreed, "no photos on the web, play it down on social media."

Dad nodded. "Ask—insist—that your friends not blab about it. For privacy's sake."

"I will keep the news away from hardened-street-tough circles," Cass said.

"Contain, concentrate, commit—that's the only way we are going to solve this genetic problem," Dad said.

No one said a word. We were all trying our hardest to avoid the great big fat imaginary elephant in the

12

room—and on its side was an imaginary sign that said HAPPY FOURTEENTH BIRTHDAY crossed out in black with a skull underneath.

"This may be the last time we see each other," Aly said in a tiny, weak, unAlylike voice.

"I will die before I let that happen to any of you," Dad replied. His face was grim, his eyes steady and fierce. "And I won't rest until my company finds a cure."

"What if they don't?" I asked.

Dad gave me a steady *have-I-ever-let-you-down?* look. "You know the McKinley family motto. It ain't over . . ."

"Until the fat lady sings." I couldn't help smiling. There were about a dozen McKinley family mottoes, and this was one of Dad's favorites.

"La-la-la," Aly sang, smiling.

Dad laughed. "Sorry, Aly, you don't fit the bill."

Cass, who hadn't spoken in a long time, finally piped up softly. "Mr. McKinley?" he said. "About number seven on your list . . . ?"

Dad smiled warmly. "That's the only one we don't have to worry about. Because it's the only item that's one hundred percent true."

CHAPTER THREE

THE ENEMY OF INTERESTING

"IT MEANS A soprano," I said, scrolling through a Wikipedia page on my trusty desktop. We'd been home for ten busy days, buying a bunk bed and a desk and a bike and clothes for Cass, catching up with teachers and friends, telling the alibi over and over a thousand times, buying hair dye to cover up the white lambda shape on the backs of our heads, blah-blah-blah. Today was going to be our first full day in school, and I was nervous. So of course it was a perfect time to procrastinate—like looking up Dad's odd saying about the singing fat lady.

"I hated that show," Cass called out from the top bunk.

"What show?" I asked.

"*The Sopranos*," Cass said. "My last foster family

binge-watched all seventeen years of it. Well, it *felt* like seventeen."

"No, I'm talking about 'the fat lady,' " I said. "It means a soprano—like, an opera singer. It's a way of saying the opera's not over until the soprano sings her big showstopping tune."

"Oh," Cass said. "What if she's not fat? The show keeps going?"

"It's a stereotype!" I said.

Cass grunted and sat up, dangling his legs over the side of the bed. "I hate stereotypes, too."

Since returning, Cass had been a thirteen-year-old curly-haired version of Dr. Jekyll and Mr. Hyde. Half the time he was his bouncy self, thanking Dad a zillion times for agreeing to adopt him. The other half he was fixated on our . . . timetable. Our predicament. Dilemma.

The fact that we were going to die.

There. I said it.

I'll admit, I hated actually putting that idea into words. I tried not to think of it as a fact. Or even think of it at all. Hey, the fat lady hadn't sung, right? Dad was trying to keep the show going.

I had to stay positive for Cass and me.

"It's weird," Cass murmured.

"What's weird?" I said.

"G7W," Cass replied.

15

"Of course it's weird," I said. "It sits in DNA for generations and then, *bam*—it shows up in people like you and me."

"No, I mean it forces us all into stereotypes," Cass said. "That always bothered me. You know, like when P. Beg called us Soldier, Sailor, Tinker, Tailor. It's like another way of saying Jock, GPS-Guy, Geek, and . . . whatever Tailor is supposed to be."

"The one who puts it all together," I said. "That's what Bhegad said."

"He slices . . . he dices . . . he figures out ways to find Loculi in ancient settings! But wait, there's more! Now the new improved Jack is also the Destroyer!" Cass let out a weary laugh. "How does that make any sense? It doesn't. At first this whole thing seemed so cool—we were going to be superhumans, woo-hoo! But the last few weeks have been like this bad dream. Don't you wish we could be normal—just kids like everybody else?"

"Cheer up, Cass," I said, scooping stuff up from my desk. "Normal is the enemy of interesting."

I dumped my pen, phone, change, and gum into my pockets. The last thing I picked up was the Loculus shard.

It was my good luck charm, I guess. For ten days I'd been carrying it with me all the time. Maybe because it reminded me of my mom. I really did believe that she had dropped it at my feet on purpose, no matter what Cass or Aly thought.

Besides, it really was awesome to look at. It felt smooth

and cool to the touch—not like metal exactly, or plastic, but dense and supertough. I held it up to the sun for a quick glance:

"You've been wearing that thing out," Cass said. "It looks like it shrunk."

"*Shrank*," I corrected him.

"Thunk you." Cass hopped down from the bunk. "Anyway, you're much more Tailor than Destroyer. That description fits Marco."

"Now who's stereotyping?" I said.

Cass giggled. "Somewhere in this world, the Massa are training Marco Ramsay to be the new king of Atlantis, while you, me, and Aly are going off to seventh grade. I think we get the better deal."

As he disappeared down the hall and into the bathroom, I heard the front doorbell ring—which seemed kind of weird for 6:39 A.M. Dropping the shard into my pocket, I glanced out the window. I saw a white minivan parked at the curb. The van's sides were emblazoned with the call letters of a local TV station WREE-TV.

Uh-oh. So much for keeping things under the radar.

"Sorry, no interviews." Dad's muffled voice echoed upward.

"We think the nation will want to hear this brave story," a woman's voice piped up. "It's got heart, grit, pathos—"

"I appreciate that," Dad said firmly. "Look, I know your station owner, Morty Reese. He'll understand as a father, we'd like our privacy."

The woman's voice got softer. "If it's compensation you're concerned about, we are prepared—"

"Compensation?" Dad shot back with a disbelieving laugh. "Wait. Morty asked you to bribe me?"

"Mr. Reese has your best interests at heart," the woman said. "This story could lead to awareness of traumatic brain injury. Hospitals will realize they need to increase security—"

"I'm sure Mr. Reese can donate directly to the hospitals if he's so concerned," Dad replied. "My private life is not for sale, sorry. Between you and me, he should learn how legitimate news organizations operate."

"Mr. Reese is an excellent newsman—" the woman protested.

"And I'm an excellent trapeze artist," Dad shot back. "Thanks but no thanks."

I heard the door shut firmly.

CHAPTER FOUR
THE BARRY

"SO, DID HE work there before or after you were born?"
Cass said as we walked up the street toward school.

"Did who work where?" I asked.

"Your dad, in the circus," Cass said. "Did you get to see
him?"

Trapeze. It took me a moment. "Dad was being sarcas-
tic," I explained. "He doesn't like Mr. Reese."

"Your dad has a weird sense of humor," Cass said.

"Reese is like the Donald Trump of Belleville," I said.
"Except with normal hair. Dad says he owns half the
town, but still Mr. Reese wants to be a media mogul.
He's the head of Reese Industries, the Bathroom Solu-
tions People."

"Whoa. As in 'Reese: The Wings Beneath Your Wind'?" Cass asked.

"Yup," I replied. "Those little plastic toilet thingies that attach the seat to the bowl. Everyone has them. That's billions in profit. And billions in profit buys local TV stations. Anyway, the most important thing is that Dad's trying to protect us. To keep our faces out of the news so he can work on saving our lives."

"Hope springs eternal," Cass said, kicking a stone up the sidewalk.

I smiled. That was the first positive thing Cass had said all day. "You know, that's one of my dad's favorite sayings."

"That's a sign!" Cass said with a grin. "I *do* belong in your family!"

I put my arm around his shoulder, and we walked quietly along a wooded area.

When Cass spoke again, his voice was soft and unsteady. "It's so hard to stay optimistic. How do you do it?"

"I try to list all the good things," I said. "Like number one, I have a new brother."

"Is there a number two?" Cass asked.

"We both feel healthy," I suggested. "We haven't needed treatments yet. Your turn."

"Um . . ." Cass replied. "Number three, it could be that this whole thing will blow over? I mean, it's possible the

Karai Institute was lying to us—you know, about needing those Sesulucol?"

"Ilucol," I corrected him.

Cass laughed. "Number four, you are getting really good at Backwardish!"

I veered off the sidewalk onto a dirt path that led into a tangle of trees that sloped downward to a creek. "Come on, this is a tuctrosh . . . tushcort . . . *shortcut.*"

"Wait—what? There's a stream down there!" Cass protested. As he walked, his foot kicked aside a busted-up baseball glove, festooned with a banana peel. "This is disgusting. Can't we take Smith Street to Whaley and then the jagged left-right on Roosevelt? Or bypass Roosevelt via the dog run?"

"Even *I* don't even know my neighborhood that well!" I said over my shoulder.

"Wait till I learn to ride a bike," Cass grumbled. "Then we'll have great options. And I won't seem like such a doofus."

"You're not a doofus," I said.

"I am the only kid in the country who can't ride a bike!" Cass replied.

"Yeah, well . . ." I said. "You had a different kind of childhood."

"As in *none*," Cass said. "You try growing up with criminal parents."

WHOOOOO . . . WHOOOO! An eerie call made me stop in my tracks.

"Cool," Cass said, bumping into me from behind. "An owl?"

Slowly a plaid shirt appeared among the rustling leaves—and then the moonlike, grinning face of Barry Reese. *"Whooooo do we have heeeere?"*

He jumped in front of us—well, if you consider slowly moving nearly two hundred pounds of well-fed and expensively dressed flesh into a narrow dirt path *jumping*.

"Not owl," I said. "Foul. Cass, meet Barry Reese."

"Son of Donald Trump?" Cass said.

Barry ignored the comment, or maybe he was too busy thinking up his next move. Barry had a hard time doing two things at once. He held up three pudgy fingers to my face, then five, then one. "How many fingers? I heard you had some mental problems, like losing your memory. Just want to test to see if you're okay, Amnesia Boy."

There were approximately three hundred middle-school kids in Belleville who would be quaking in their boots at this kind of bullying. But after facing up to killer zombies, sharp-taloned griffins, and acid-spitting vizzeet, I wasn't bothered by Barry Reese. "Stick two of them into your eyes and I'll count slowly," I said.

He shoved both of us backward. His face was covered with a sheen of sweat as he grinned sadistically at Cass.

"Look! It's Cash! The hardened LA stweet tough who still wides a twicycle!"

"Wait, how did you know that?" Cass said.

"Um, maybe because you just announced it to the world?" Barry replied. "Can I have your autograph? It's okay if you want to use cwayons."

I lunged forward and gave Barry a shove. "It's *Cass*. And he only gives autographs to people who know how to read."

Unfortunately pushing a guy of Barry's bulk was like trying to move a boulder. He bumped me hard with his belly and grabbed my backpack straps. "That was disrespectful, McKinley. The Barry sent you to the hospital once and he can do it again. Now give me your phone."

"My *phone*?" I said. "Doesn't the Barry have a phone?"

His beefy fingers were already in my jeans pocket. As I wriggled to get away, the pocket popped inside out along with Barry's hand. All my stuff spilled out onto the ground, including the Loculus shard.

Cass and I scrambled to grab it, but Barry was shockingly fast when he was excited. "What's this?" he asked, scrunching up his face at the shard.

"Nothing!" I blurted.

"Then why did you both grab for it first?" As he lifted it upward, the shard glinted in the sunlight. "What's that weird star shape on it? A symbol from a secret nerd society?"

"Mathletes!" Cass said. "It's . . . a club. Of math people. We talk about . . . pi. And stuff like that."

"I like pies, too . . . but I don't like *lies*!" Barry snickered at his own idiotic joke. "Especially lies about anti-American world-domination cults that kidnap kids for weeks at a time!"

Cass was shaking now. "Jack, is he going loony tunes on us? Should we be calling nine-one-one?"

Barry stepped closer, his beady eyes shifting from me to Cass. "You're not a street tough, Casper, are you? And, Jack, you didn't lose your memory and travel across the country. Your little story? It's full of holes. My dad thinks your dad has connections with terrorists. Where does he fly all the time? What's with all the long trips to Magnolia?"

"Mongolia," Cass corrected him.

"Wait—*terrorists*?" I said. "There are no terrorists in Mongolia!"

"Ha—so you *were* there!" Barry said.

"My dad runs a genetics lab there," I replied. Barry's face went blank, so I added, "That's the study of genes, and not the kind you wear."

Barry grabbed my shoulder and turned me around. He cradled the back of my head in his right hand. "Where's the white hair, Jack?"

"*What?*" I squeaked.

He let go of my head and spun me back around. "That

day you fell into the street—I saw this, like, upside-down V shape on the back of your head. Now it's gone. It means something, doesn't it? A secret symbol from some hidden organization?"

Cass's eyes were huge. Leave it to Barry, the dumbest person I knew, to come the closest to the truth.

"Uh . . ." Cass said.

"I'm right, huh?" Barry barked. "Go ahead, tell the Barry he's right!"

Let your enemy give you the lead.

Dad had recited that one to me at least a thousand times. And now, in this moment, I finally understood it.

I stepped right up to Barry and refused to blink. Then I took a deep breath and spoke fast. "You want the truth? Okay. My hair and Cass's? Yup, it did go white in the back, in the shape of a Greek lambda, which is their letter *L*. Now our hair is dyed. The lambda means we inherited a gene from a prince who escaped the sinking of Atlantis. See, the gene unlocks part of our DNA that turns our best ability into a superpower. But it also overwhelms the body, and no one who's ever had it has lived past the age of fourteen. In the last year of life, the body begins to break down. You get sick every few weeks. You can stay alive for a while if you get certain treatments, but eventually you die. We learned this from a group called the Karai Institute on this island that can't be detected. They told us we can be cured if we find seven magical Loculi that contain the power of Atlantis, which were hidden centuries ago in the Seven Wonders of the Ancient World. As you know—well, maybe you don't—six of the Wonders don't exist anymore. The thing in your hand is a piece of a destroyed Loculus."

"Jack?" Cass mouthed, as if I'd just lost my mind.

Barry's mouth was sagging. His eyes narrowed, as if he were still stuck on the second sentence. Which he probably was.

Would he try to repeat his own mangled version of what I'd just said to his dad? I hoped so, because any sane human being would send him straight to a psychologist. And he knew it.

"Well, that's everything," I said, reaching to grab the Loculus from Barry's hand.

He pulled it back.

"Okay, so if you're supposed to get sick every few weeks . . ." he said quietly, "how come you're not sick?"

"The fresh, rejuvenating Belleville air?" Cass said.

Barry's face curled. "You guys are playing me. That was the obvious-est lie! I'm going to get to the bottom of this. You watch, I'll find out the truth."

"Great," I said. "Meanwhile, will you give me that back?"

"Why should I give you a piece of a destroyed Oculus?" Barry asked. "It might be worth something."

"Loculus," Cass said. "With an *L*."

"Trust me," I said, "it's worth absolutely nothing to you."

"Awwww, really?" Barry said. "Nothing?"

With an exasperated sigh, Barry held out the shard to Cass. Both of us reached for it at the same time.

Before our fingers could touch it, Barry spun away. With a grunt, he tossed it far into the scrubby, trash-strewn woods.

"Fetch," he said. "With an *F*."

CHAPTER FIVE

SHARD LUCK

"WHAT HAPPENED TO your face?" Dad stared at me oddly, standing in the front door.

I peeked past him to the sofa, where a strange man dressed in black was rising to his feet. "Thorns," I said, touching my cheek, where the edges of thin gash peeked out from behind a Band-Aid. "We lost something in the woods."

I didn't want to mention the shard in front of a stranger. It had taken us about a half hour on our hands and knees in the woods to find it. Which made us very late for school. The cool thing was, no one seemed to care. Cass and I were like returning war heroes. Everyone was nice to us. The nurse cleaned us up and gave me a whole box of Band-Aids.

29

The principal herself, Mrs. Sauer (pronounced *Sour*), brought a Welcome Back cake into homeroom. Barry ate most of it, but it was still nice. I even had a session with the school psychologist, who said she was screening me for PTSD. At first I thought that was some kind of a sandwich, like pastrami, turkey, salami, and dark bread, but it means post–traumatic stress disorder. The only stress I felt was from thinking about the great sandwich I wasn't going to eat.

"Jack . . . Cass," Dad said, "this is Mr. Anthony from Lock-Tite Security. After that strange little visit from the TV station this morning, I figure we'd better make ourselves safe from intrusions, wiretaps, recording devices. Somebody in this town—who shall remain nameless—thinks he's going to win an Emmy Award for investigative journalism."

Cass nodded. "I understand, Mr. McKinley. I met his son. I don't blame you."

"We'll go upstairs," I said.

We raced each other through the living room and up the back stairs. Cass reached the second-floor landing first. He quickly tossed off his shoes and socks before walking on the Oriental rug that lined the long hallway. "I love the way this feels. This house is so cool."

"You could have a whole room of your own, you know," I said. "We have a lot of them. There's more on third floor, too."

"We already decided we were going to share," Cass said. "Are you changing your mind?"

"No!" I said. "I just thought . . . if you ever felt like you needed space. It's a big house and all."

Cass shook his head, his face darkening. "Besides we have to be prepared. We can't be separated if it happens . . ."

"*It?*" I said.

"You know . . . *it*," Cass repeated. "Dying."

I leaned over, softly banging my head on the wood railing that looked out onto the first floor vestibule. "I thought we talked about this. We're going to stay positive, remember? We're feeling good so far, Dad is on the case—"

"Right," Cass said. "But doesn't that first part seem scary to you? About us feeling good?"

"*Dying* is scary, Cass!" I said. "Feeling good is not scary!"

"But we shouldn't be feeling good!" Cass replied. "By now, both of us—or at least you—should have had an episode. Which would mean we'd need a treatment. No one knows how to give us one!"

"Dad is working on it," I said.

"He has no contact with anyone in the KI, so how can he figure it out?" Cass said. "I've been thinking all day about what Barry Reese said. Why are we still healthy, Jack? We shouldn't be!"

"Uh, guys?" Dad's face appeared directly below me. He was scowling. "Can you please take it inside?"

Cass and I ran into our room and shut the door tight. I emptied my pockets onto the desk, yanked off my ripped pants, and quickly pulled on a pair of sweats I'd left on the floor. That was another agreement Cass and I had made. I could keep my side of the room as messy as I wanted.

Feeling more comfortable, I began pacing. "Okay, let's think about this. The intervals are irregular. Always have been. We know that."

"Yeah, but the older we get, the *closer* they should be," Cass said.

I couldn't argue that. Professor Bhegad had warned us exactly that would happen as we neared the Day of Doom.

Closer. Not farther away.

"I think it's the shards," Cass said. "Remember, it was the Loculus of *Healing*. It was supposed to restore life to the dead."

"You mean *shard*," I said.

"Shards." Cass shrugged. "I took one, too."

I looked at him. "You did? Why didn't you tell me?"

"I didn't think it was important," Cass replied. "I just took it as a souvenir. It's not as nice as yours. No designs or anything. I thought it was just a busted, useless piece of junk. But now . . ."

He went to his desk and pulled open a drawer. From the bottom he took out a hunk of material maybe three inches long, wrapped in tissue. "It's kind of ugly."

32

I heard a rustling noise from my pile of junk on my desk and jumped away.

Cass dropped the shard. "Whoa. Did you bring in a *mouse?*"

The rustling stopped. I darted my hand out and pushed aside some candy wrappers. No critters there.

Just my shard.

"Pick it up, Cass," I said softly. "Your shard."

Cass swallowed. He lifted the little disklike thing from the floor. On the desk, my shard began to twitch like a jumping bean. "Whoa . . ." Cass said.

I leaned over, peering closely at my shard, then Cass's. "They're not two random pieces," I said. "It looks like they may have broken apart from each other."

"It feels warm," Cass said.

"Hold the long side toward me," I said.

As Cass angled his arm, I reached out to my shard and turned it so its longest side faced Cass's.

"Ow—it's like a hundred degrees!" Cass said.

"Hold tight!" I said.

I felt a jolt like an electric current. As I pulled my fingers away from the shard, it shot across the room toward Cass.

With a scream, he dropped his relic and jumped away.

Bluish-white light flashed across our room. As Cass fell back on the lower bed with a shriek, the two shards collided in midair with a loud *DZZZZZT* and a blast that smelled like rotten eggs.

Flames shot up from the carpet as the pieces landed. I raced to the bathroom for a glass of water and doused the small fire quickly. I could hear Dad yelling at us from downstairs.

But neither Cass nor I answered him. We were too busy staring at what remained in the singed, smoking patch of carpet.

Not two shards, but one.

They had joined together, without a seam.

CHAPTER SIX
ALY-BYE

"WAIT, THEY JUST flew together and joined in midair," Aly said, "like snowflakes?"

Her hair was purple now, her face pale on my laptop screen. Belleville, Indiana, may have been overcast, but the Los Angeles sunshine was pouring through Aly's bedroom window.

"It was more like massive colliding spacecraft," Cass said. "Only . . . tiny. And not in outer space."

I held up the joined sections. Together they formed one larger shard. "You can't even tell where they were separated."

"That's awesome," Aly replied, as her face loomed closer to the screen. "Absomazingly ree-donculous. It means that—"

Aly turned away from the screen and let out a loud sneeze.

And then another.

Cass's eyes widened. "Are you okay?"

"A cold," Aly said.

"Because Jack and I were wondering, you know, about the treatments," Cass went on. "It's been a while since your last episode . . ."

"It's *a cold*, that's all," Aly said, clacking away at her laptop. "Let's get down to business. I've been doing research. Tons. About the Seven Wonders. About Atlantis."

"Why?" Cass asked.

"Because what else am I going to do?" Aly said. "I know you're feeling bad, Cass. But I refuse to give up. We start by trying to get back in touch with the KI. They're lying low, but I'm betting they'll want to be in contact with us. Which means we need to protect our alibi. So I pretended to be, like, an evil spy searching for clues to break our story. All kinds of things didn't add up. That doctor friend of your dad's? His employee records showed he was in Mexico the day he supposedly treated Cass. And the convenience store where Marco was last seen? Its video feed showed a seven-foot-tall, red-bearded barefoot guy who bought three peanut butter sandwiches and a dozen doughnuts. The owner was suspicious, so he sent the feed to the local cops, who ran a primitive facial ID scan. They came up with three hundred and seven possible suspects. Including one Victor Rafael Quiñones."

"Who's that?" Cass asked.

"*Tor* from Victor, *quin* from Quiñones," Aly said. "I'm figuring Torquin is a nickname."

"Wait. His name is *Victor*?" Cass said.

"So of course I deleted the footage of Torquin from the FTP servers," Aly said. "Even the backups. And I altered the doctor's hospital records, too. I even hacked into his Facebook account and deleted the pictures of Mexico. I am covering our tracks so the alibi is clean. But the point is, I can't do everything. Things can go wrong. What if there are off-line copies of the originals? *Arrrrrghh!*" Aly shook her fists in frustration. "Okay. Okay, Black, stay calm and hack. I will try to locate Torquin or anyone who seems connected to the KI."

"Is that possible?" Cass asked.

Aly shrugged. "Anything's—" She broke off in a fit of coughing, swinging away from the screen. All we saw now was her bookcase.

"Aly?" Cass said.

Something thumped. I heard a choking noise. A pounding on the floor. *"Mo-o-om!"* came Aly's voice.

A blur passed across the screen—a woman with salt-and-pepper hair, wearing a T-shirt and jeans. She passed from top to bottom, falling to her knees and out of the screen. "Aly? *Aly, wake up!*"

I was on my feet now. *"ALY!"*

The image on the screen juddered. And then all went black.

CHAPTER SEVEN

DOWN AND OUT IN LA

"GALLUP, MCKINLEY!" CASS said, staring out the window of the jet.

"I'm not piloting this plane, Captain Nied is," Dad replied. "And he's going as fast as he can."

"That's not what I meant." Cass gestured to the distant ground below, which was clearly visible even in the dimming sunlight. "That little town near the river? It's called Gallup, New Mexico. Right near the Arizona border. It also happens to be in McKinley County. So it's Gallup, McKinley."

I took a deep breath. I could barely focus on what Cass what saying. Except for the "Gallup" part. Because my heart was galloping.

"I think it's named for US president William McKinley," Cass said. "He was shot. But he didn't die right away. He died because no one got to him in time."

"That's cheerful," Captain Nied said.

"Cass," Dad said softly, "we're doing the best we can. We'll get to Aly. She's with the best doctors in Southern California. Dr. Karl has promised me she'll see to her personally."

Dr. Karl was another college friend of Dad's. She was the head of emergency medicine at St. Dunstan Hospital, where Aly had been taken. I was becoming convinced Dad knew at least half the doctors in the United States. In my left hand I clutched my phone. Before leaving, I'd sent Aly three unanswered texts. There was no cell reception up here, but that didn't stop me from looking at the screen for about the thousandth time.

In my right hand I turned the shard around and around as if it were a magic charm. As if I could somehow massage it to full size. "I wish we were taking her a whole Loculus of Healing."

"That wouldn't cure her," Cass said. "Or us. It takes seven of these things to do that."

"Yeah, but it would buy some time," I said.

"You and I are feeling fine without a Loculus of Healing," Cass remarked with a deep sigh. "Why us and not her? Why does she get the bad luck?"

I stopped turning the shard. My hands felt warm. My first thought was body heat.

My second thought was, *Are you* crazy?

Spoons and forks didn't heat up in your hands when you fiddled with them. Neither did joysticks, worry beads, action figures, whatever.

I handed it to Cass. "Notice anything?"

"Whoa," Cass said. "Do you have a fever or something?"

"It's warm, right?" I said. "Like, unnaturally warm?"

Cass turned it around curiously. "It looks smaller to me."

"Cass, what if that heat isn't just heat?" I said. "What if it means something—like, it's active in some way?"

"Like, alive?" Cass said.

"No!" I said. "It's the shell of a Loculus that's existed for thousands of years, right? What if it absorbed some of that healing power? Maybe that's what's keeping you and me from having episodes."

Cass's eyes were as wide as baseballs. Dad was staring at the shard, too, from the copilot's seat. Together we looked at Captain Nied.

He yanked back the throttle, and the jet began to dive. "Fasten your seat belts, gents. And welcome to LA."

* * *

It is amazing what $200 will do to a Los Angeles cab-driver.

As we twisted and turned through the city streets, palm

40

trees and white stucco houses zoomed by in a blur. We could see the freeway in the distance, the cars at a total standstill. "Freeway is not free!" the cabdriver said in an accent I couldn't quite figure out. "Is prison for cars!"

No one laughed. We were too busy keeping our stomachs from jumping through our mouths. Dad was on his cell phone with the hospital the whole way.

According to Dr. Karl, Aly was alive, but it wasn't looking good.

As the taxi screeched to a stop in the hospital parking lot, we pushed our way out. I hooked my backpack around my shoulders and sprinted after Dad. He flashed his ID left and right, fast-talking his way past guards. In a moment we were on the fifth floor, barging into the intensive care unit. It was a massive room, echoing with beeps and shouts and lined with curtained-off areas.

A dark-haired woman with huge eyes peered out from behind one of the curtains. "How is she, Cindy?" Dad asked, marching across the room as if he were a regular.

"Breathing," Dr. Karl said, "but unresponsive. Her fever is spiking around a hundred four."

I pulled the shard out of my pocket and held tight. I almost didn't recognize Aly. Her skin was ashen, her eyes were only half-open, and her hair was pulled back into a green hospital cap. A breathing tube snaked from her mouth to a machine against the wall, and a tangle of tubes connected her arm to an IV stand with three different fluids.

Over her head was a screen that showed her heartbeat on a graph.

Aly's mom was holding her daughter's hand. Her face was streaked with tears, and her narrow glasses had slipped down her nose. She looked startled to see us. "Doctor . . . ?"

"Sorry," Dr. Karl said, "I'm going to have to ask the kids to stay in the waiting room. Standard procedure for intensive care."

"I have to speak to her," I insisted.

"She won't hear you," Aly's mom said. "She's completely unresponsive."

"Can I just touch her?" I said.

"*Touch* her?" Mrs. Black looked at me as if I were crazy.

"This is way beyond ICU protocol," Dr. Karl said. "If you don't leave now, I will have to call security—"

BEEP! BEEP! BEEP!

Cass and I jumped back. "Are they coming to get us?" Cass asked.

"It's not a security alarm. It's something to do with Aly!" I said. Aly's monitors were flashing red. Her eyes sprang open and then rolled upward into her head. She let out a choking sound, and her body began to twitch. As three nurses came running from the center of the room, Dr. Karl strapped Aly's arms down.

"What's happening?" I demanded.

"Febrile seizure!" Dr. Karl said. *"Clear the area!"*

"But—" I said.

A nurse with a barrel chest and a trim beard pulled me back, and I nearly collided with Cass. As the hospital staff closed in around Aly's bed, we both stumbled back toward the entrance.

"They're killing her, Jack!" Cass said. "Do something!"

I dropped my pack. "I'm going invisible. It's the only way I can get to her."

"There's no room for you," Cass said. "If you barge in, they will feel you, Jack. It'll freak everybody out. Total chaos, and it won't be good for her."

"Any other ideas?" I said.

Cass nodded. "Yeah. I'll distract them. Give me three seconds."

"What?"

But Cass was already running away, heading toward the table that contained the medical equipment and monitors.

One . . .

I reached into the pack and lifted out the Loculus of Invisibility.

Two . . .

As I stepped forward, the loud beeps stopped. I looked toward the monitors. They were dark. Aly's equipment had shut down completely. Cass was scampering away from the wall socket, where he had pulled out the plugs.

Three!

I heard a shout. Two nurses broke away from Aly, scrambling toward the equipment, leaving her right side wide open. I raced toward her, clutching the Loculus of Invisibility with one hand and the shard with the other. Dr. Karl was injecting something into her left arm, concentrating hard.

Aly's chest was still. She wasn't breathing. I placed the shard on her stomach, just below her ribs.

"The pads—now!" Dr. Karl shouted. "We're losing her!"

"Come on . . ." I said under my breath. "Come on, Aly. You have to live." Aly's eyes stared upward, green and bright, dancing in the light even in her unconsciousness. I felt like I could talk to her, like she'd answer me back with some kind of geeky joke. I wanted to see her smile.

But there was no reaction. Not a fraction of an inch of movement.

A doctor was racing toward Aly with two pads strapped to his hands. They were going to try to shock her alive. I pressed the shard harder into her abdomen. I guess I was crying, because tears were falling onto her face.

Aly's mom bumped into me and screamed. It wouldn't be much longer before my invisible presence was going to be a big deal.

"We have power!" a voice barked. With a soft whoosh, the monitors fired up and the lights blinked on. The

44

heartbeat graph showed a long, horizontal, flat line.

Dead. A flat line meant dead.

The doctor placed the pads on either side of Aly's chest but I did not take my hand away—not even when they shot electricity through her, and her body flopped like a rag doll.

It wasn't working.

Aly was ghost white and still. Her chest wasn't moving. As Dr. Karl finally called off the electric shocks, I pressed harder than ever, leaning toward her face.

"I'm . . . I'm so, so sorry," Dr. Karl said to Aly's mom.

I had failed.

She was the first to die. One of us would be next, then the other. And then there would be none.

I brushed my lips against her cool forehead. "Good-bye, Aly," I whispered. "I—" The words clogged up in my brain, and I had to force them out. "I love you, dude. Yeah. Just saying."

I let go of her and walked away toward the center of the room. I felt numb. My eyes focused on nothing.

"Jack?" Cass whispered, wandering toward me, looking all teary and confused. "Where are you?"

I picked up the backpack and slipped the Loculus of Invisibility back inside. As I became visible, I noticed I was next to two doctors who must have seen me materialize out of thin air.

But they hadn't seemed to notice. They were both

staring over my head toward Aly. Gaping.

Cass turned. His jaw dropped. "What the—?"

As I wiped away tears, the first thing I noticed was Aly's mom. She was on the floor, fainted away.

The second thing I noticed was Aly sitting up, staring straight at me.

"You *love* me?" she said.

CHAPTER EIGHT

THE HUMPTY DUMPTY PROJECT

SHE WAS ALIVE.

Half of me wanted to jump with joy. The other half wanted to sink down and melt into the linoleum. Dad and Dr. Karl stood by the bed, gaping as if their mouths had been propped open by invisible pencils.

"I heard you say it, Jack McKinley!" Aly laughed as if nothing bad had happened. "You said, 'I love you'! I heard it!"

My mouth flapped open and shut a couple of times. "The shard . . ." I finally squeaked. "It worked."

Aly's smile abruptly vanished. She looked around the ICU. "Wait. *Jack? Cass?* What are you doing here? Why am I in a hospital? Why is Mom on the floor?"

I rushed over. Dad and I both lifted Mrs. Black to

her feet. Her eyes puddled with tears. As she hugged her daughter, the place was going nuts. Cass was screaming, pumping his fists. The hospital staff high-fived each other like middle school kids. Dr. Karl looked bewildered. I thought I could see some tears on her cheeks as Aly's mom hugged her, too.

"You are a miracle worker, doctor," Mrs. Black said. "Thank you."

"I—I'm not sure what did it," Dr. Karl said. "I guess . . . the pads?"

Aly pulled me closer. "What happened?" she whispered. "I had an episode, right? And you guys flew out to see me."

"Um, yeah," I whispered back.

"So how did the doctor figure out—?" she asked.

"She didn't," I replied.

"Wait—so *you* did it?" she said. "You saved my life?"

"It's a long story," I said.

Aly smiled. Her eyes moistened. "Backsies."

"What?"

"About what you said," she said, "into my ear . . ."

I felt my face heating up. "That's because I thought you were dead!"

Doofus. Idiot.

She was looking at me like I'd just slapped her. But before either of us could say anything, the crowd of medical people began elbowing me away. Dr. Karl was shouting orders. All kinds of tubes were being hooked up to Aly's arms.

I backed away, standing with Cass. "Boj emosewa," he said.

"Thanks," I said.

I took a deep breath. I felt a million things. Happiness. Relief. Embarrassment. Pride. I could finally feel my body relaxing. That was when I opened my clenched palm and looked at the shard.

It was the size of a quarter.

And the only thing I felt was scared.

* * *

"What if it just . . . vanishes?" Cass paced back and forth in our hotel room. Behind him was a huge picture window. The sunset looked like an egg yolk spreading on the Pacific Ocean. "We use up its power, it gets smaller and smaller, and then, poof, it's gone?"

"I wasn't expecting it to shrink like that," I said.

"Jack, it's been getting smaller all along," Cass said. "I tried to tell you that back home. It must be like a battery. You and I used up some of its power. Aly used up a lot more."

"We have to preserve it somehow," I said. "But we can't exactly hide it away. It's buying us time."

"I wish we could contact the KI," Cass said with a sigh. "I wish we hadn't been cut off like that. Don't you think that's weird—they take Torquin away and then . . . radio silence?"

"Maybe they've given up on us," I said.

Cass flopped on one of the double beds and stared out the window. "Now you sound like me."

I could feel my phone vibrating in my pocket. Aly was calling. "Hello?" I said.

"I'm bored," Aly's voice piped up.

I put her on speaker. "Hi, Bored. I'm Jack. Cass is here, too. How are you feeling?"

"Good," she replied. "Too good to be sitting here in the dark in a hospital room. The doctors have finally stopped coming in and gawking. They're talking about releasing me tomorrow. I'm like the Miracle Girl. I feel like an exhibit at the Museum of Natural Hysteria, and I'm tired of talking. So it's your turn, Jack. *You* know what happened to me, and I want you to tell me now."

I explained it all—the shards, the shrinkage, the healing power, the trip to LA, and my stunt with the Loculus of Invisibility.

When I was done, the phone fell quiet for a long moment. "Um, are you still awake?" I finally said.

"That silence," she said, "is the sound of my mind being blown. Do you realize what this means? If your two shards fused like that, we may be able to put the whole thing together again."

"Like Humpty Dumpty!" Cass added.

"Which means we have to get to the other pieces," Aly went on.

Cass hopped off the bed. *"Yes!"*

"Whoa, hold on—the Massa took the other pieces," I said. "They're probably back on the island right now, trying to fit them together."

"Exactly," Aly said. "So there are two possibilities. They manage to do it, and they realize there's a piece missing. In which case they will be coming after us."

"Or?" I said.

"Or they won't be able to do anything with those shards at all," she said, "because you guys are G7W and they're not. Don't forget, the Loculi get their power from us. Without us, there's a good chance those shards will just be shards."

"You are a genius," Cass said.

"How do we get to the island?" I said. "My dad can get us anywhere from Chicago to Kathmandu in a private plane. But even he can't get to an island shielded from detection. Torquin's the only person who can get us there, and he's gone."

"It's findable by the KI, and by the Massa," Aly said. "If they can do it, so can we."

"How?" Cass asked.

"I'm thinking," Aly said.

I was thinking, too. I was thinking about Brother Dimitrios and my mom, heading across the ocean. Dimitrios was probably happy to have the Loculus pieces. Maybe the Massa couldn't fuse the shards, but they could try to fit them together like puzzle pieces. Would Dimitrios find out that Mom had dropped one? What would happen to her if he did?

I began to sweat. Even now, I wasn't sure which side Mom was on. She seemed to want to help us. Which would make her a mole inside the Massa organization. But she had left Dad and me to join them—faked her own death and kept it secret all these years. How could I trust her? *How could I not trust my own mom?*

My mind was firing in all directions. I pictured Mom on a plane with the Massa, staring out the window, scared.

"The Massa," I said. "Somehow we have to get the Massa to take us there."

"Are you crazy?" Cass said. "We just risked our lives escaping them!"

"Jack, we don't know where they are," Aly said.

Something Dad had said on the train was still echoing in my head. *The best way to predict how people will act is knowing what they want.*

"Maybe not," I said. "But we know what they want. And it's the same thing the KI wants."

"World domination?" Cass asked.

"Loculi," I replied. "And we still have two of them. At some point—probably after the heat is off us—they will come after us."

"We don't have time to wait," Aly said. "It may take

them weeks, or months. That shard is going to shrink to nothing."

"Exactly," I said. "We have to make that happen ourselves. We have to make them find us. There are four likely places they are monitoring right now—four places that have the unfound Loculi."

"The four remaining Wonders of the World!" Aly blurted out.

"I'll work on my dad," I said. "You work on your mom, Aly. Explain that it's a matter of life or death. We get ourselves back to the island and find Fiddle. He's hidden away with some KI operatives. They've got to be planning something. They'll help us. The moment you get out of the hospital—"

"Wait," Cass said. "We're supposed to sneak away, travel to one of the sites, and look for the Massa?"

"No." I shook my head. "All we need to do is go there. And let them come to us."

CHAPTER NINE

MAUSOLEUM DREAM

I LOOK OVER my shoulder. He is not here yet. But he will be.

WHO?

All I know, all I recognize, is that I am back in Bodrum. The last place in the world I want to be. The place where we failed to find the Loculus. Our last stop before NYC, where all our hope was lost—

The others—Dad, Cass, Aly, Torquin, and Canavar—are nowhere. The hotels and houses are gone, too. I'm wearing sandals and a robe. My mind goes from confusion to panic. Before me is an expanse of blackness, the contours of surrounding hills lit only by moonlight.

Bodrum is Halicarnassus. I am in another time. And my Jack thoughts are being crowded out of my head.

In rushes a flood of other, more distant memories. Of beauty and pain. Of deep-green forests and smooth blue lakes, happy laughing families, scholars teaching children, athletes wrestling deadly piglike vromaskis, sharp-clawed red griffins swooping overhead.

Of smoldering clouds and raging fires, blackened corpses and shrieking beasts.

Over my shoulder is a leather sack. Inside is a sphere. It looks like the Loculus of Healing, but I know it's not. It is fake. I planned it this way. I am also heading in the wrong direction—away from the distant silhouette of the great half-finished structure in the distance. The Mausoleum.

I planned that part, too.

I hurry onward quickly, keeping the sea to my left.

I know now. I am Massarym. And I have a plan.

Not far ahead, maybe a half mile, is a hill. Trees and thick bushes. A team of mercenaries awaits there. They will take me to safety. After my plan is fulfilled.

I want to be found before I reach them. I must be found. The plan depends on this. My mind conjures up an image: the real Loculus, I see, is safe underground. Or so I hope.

I am scared. But I slow my steps, deepen my breaths.

When the explosion happens, I am barely prepared for the blast of light, the cloud of dirt like a giant fist. I stagger back. I fall to my knees.

Then the cloud begins to lift, and a tall, bearded man emerges. He wears a white, gilt-edged robe. Although his hair is gray, he stands straight, like a warrior, his shoulders thickly muscled. His *body radiates power, but his face, which is familiar to me, is etched in sadness.*

Part of me wants to run to him, to hug him. But those days are over. The lines have been drawn. He is my enemy now, because he is an enemy of the world.

"I am hoping you have come to your senses," he says deeply, forcefully.

I am both comforted and repulsed by the sound of my father's voice.

As the old man comes nearer, his robe snaps in the sea-thick wind. I see the hilt of his sword, his prized possession, jutting from its scabbard. But the scabbard's leather is frayed and ragged looking. I know Father must not be happy about this indignity. Slowly I sidestep closer to the edge of the cliff. Below us, the waves crash against the shore.

"My senses," I say in a voice with false confidence, a voice that isn't my own, "have never been lost, Uhla'ar."

The old man's face softens slightly into a rueful smile. He holds out a powerful arm, his palm extended.

I step closer and then turn. With a swift, sure thrust, I toss the Loculus into the sea.

I watch the sphere turning and growing smaller in the dull light of the moon. My father's eyes bulge. His mouth becomes a black hole.

As he dives into the raging churn below, his scream slices me like a dagger.

CHAPTER TEN

IF IT LOOKS LIKE A HOAX . . . ?

TWO DAYS.

That was how long it took the doctors to release Aly. I thought about the dream a lot during that time. But neither Cass nor I could figure out what it meant.

The more important thing was convincing Dad about our plan. He tried hard to act like we were happy beach-going tourists in la-la land, but we pounded him with logic and pleading, to no avail. I'm surprised he didn't drop us both into the La Brea Tar Pits.

When Aly was released, we had a great reunion, on two levels. On the top floor of her house, Aly, Cass, and I pored over her research materials, trying to figure out where to get ourselves captured.

On the first floor, her mom and my dad were having lunch. And arguing. Well, okay, *discussing*.

"My dad doesn't love the idea," I said.

"He's gone from 'Are you out of your minds?' to 'Can we change the subject?'" Cass said.

"I think Mom is willing," Aly said. "I told her this was the only way to keep me alive. She said she'd already seen me die and didn't want it to happen again. Give her a chance. She can be very persuasive." Her fingers clicked over the keyboard. "Okay, take a look at this."

www.magicalRouthouni.gr

EXPERIENSE THE
MAGICK OF ANCIENT
ROUTHOUNI

• With it's healing waters and cultures of great marvell, that makes Routhouni famous!!!

• Dine in style with so many of our delictious caffés by the water side!!!!!

• While the ancient Wonder Of The World. "KING ZEUS" who every one talks of throgh all histories, waethes over YOU!!!!!

"Looks like Torquin on a bad hair day," Cass said.

"Is this a joke?" I asked.

"Stay with me," Aly said. "I thought this was cheesy, too, but there was something about it. So I did a little digging around. And I found this."

Now she was clicking away to another page:

MYTHDEBUNKERS.org
Exposing hoaxes since 1998

Statue in Routhouni Square, Greece,
Is the Statue of Zeus at Olympia

FALSE.
An email message has been circulating since 2001, citing an archaeological claim that a statue in a small Peloponnesian town is actually one of the Seven Wonders of the Ancient World: the Statue of Zeus at Olympia.

THE LEGEND: The statue appeared in an olive grove near Routhouni in AD 425, around the time of the demise of the statue of Zeus. At the statue's feet was the dead body of a young man, impaled by Zeus's staff. Amazed locals brought the statue into town, convinced it was a manifestation of Zeus himself. With proper honor and worship, they thought, Zeus would remain a silent and benevolent protector.

THE FACTS: the statue in Routhouni Square looks nothing like the statue of Zeus, which was seated. Its obvious crudeness strikes many as laughable. Some nineteenth-century scholars claimed it was a study for the Zeus statue, or perhaps the statue's "first draft." But in the face of no evidence, modern scholars conclude that this is old-fashioned Victorian thinking at its most fanciful.

I took a deep breath. "If it looks like a hoax and the experts say it's a hoax . . ."

Aly clicked the back button and returned to the Routhouni website. "Take a look at the thing in the statue's hand."

She zoomed in to the image:

"A bowling ball?" Cass said.

Aly smacked him. "What if it's a *Loculus*? Think about it. The Seven Wonders were built to protect the Loculi. When we found the Colossus, he tried to kill us. What if the statue of Zeus came to life, too?"

"So it went after somebody who tried to take its Loculus, stabbed him, then went back to being a statue?" Cass asked. "Who would try to take a Loculus? Who would even know what it was?"

"Another Select, I guess," I said with a shrug.

"So Zeus the statue came to life and went after the thief," Aly said. "He actually transformed into Zeus the god. And he chased the thief until he caught up to him. After killing the thief, Zeus turned back into a statue."

Cass gave her a dubious smile. "Okay, that's one possibility. What about the other Wonders?"

"Well, there's the Lighthouse at Pharos," she said, "but that's in Alexandria, which is a big bustling city—too exposed. The Temple of Artemis is in a big tourist area—Ephesus, Turkey. We've been to the Pyramids, and we know the Massa cleared out of there. I think Zeus is our best shot. Look, the question is not *Is this convincing?* The question is *Would the Massa think this is convincing?* I'm betting yes. I'm betting they have this thing staked out."

Before she finished the sentence, I could hear footsteps on the stairs.

We froze. Dad and Mrs. Black appeared in the doorway. Their faces were grim and drawn. Dad had his phone in his hand. I could practically read the *no* in their eyes.

I decided to talk first.

"January, August, April, July," I said. "Those are the months Aly, Marco, Cass, and I turn fourteen. I know what you're going to say, Dad. MGL is hard at work on a cure. But—"

"We had a setback at McKinley Genetics Lab," Dad

said. "Our team was developing a shutoff mechanism. But it doesn't work. The gene mutates, Jack. When you attach anything to its receptors, they change shape. It's like a beast that grows a new heart after you kill it."

"That so totally sucks," Cass said.

"What does it mean?" I asked.

Dad sighed. "It means we'll need six months of new research, maybe a year . . ."

I felt the blood drain from my face. "We don't have that time."

Aly's mom ran her fingers through her daughter's hair. "No, you don't."

Dad nodded. "We're going back to the hotel. How long will it take you to be ready, Aly?"

"Five minutes!" Aly shot back. "Maybe four."

Dad turned toward the door and said the words I hadn't expected to hear. "Wheels up in one hour. Wherever you guys want to go."

CHAPTER ELEVEN

GOD OF COUCH POTATOES

LEAVING THE LOCULI at home was out of the question. Dad and I were both paranoid the Massa—or some snoop hired by Morty Reese—would break in and steal them. So we took them with us on Dad's jet. For protection. We also packed flashlights and supplies in our packs and made sure our phones were charged.

The ride was bumpy. We argued for six hours about how to proceed. Aly was still thin and quiet from being sick. But by the time we reached the Kalamata International Airport, we had a plan. Cass, Aly, and I would grab a taxi. Alone. Bringing Dad with us, we decided, would make the Massa suspicious. Plus, it would do us no good if he wound up captured along with us.

So Dad and the Loculi stayed behind with the plane.

I was a nervous wreck. The taxi had no air-conditioning and there was a hole in the front passenger floor. Rocks spat up into the car from the road as we sped noisily across Greece. Soon the mountains of the Peloponnese rose up in the distance to our right, and Cass had a revelation. "Whoa," he cried out, looking up from his phone. "The meaning of *Routhouni* is 'nostril'!"

"Is geography!" our driver said. (Everything he said seemed to come with an exclamation point.) "Just north of Routhouni is long mountain with—how do you say? Ridge! To Ancient Greeks, this looks like straight nose! Greek nose! Strong! At bottom is two valleys—round valleys! Is like, you know . . . *thio Routhounia* . . . two nostrils!"

"And thus," Cass announced, "Routhouni *picked* its name."

"Cass, please . . ." Aly said.

Cass began narrating like a TV host. "Our car develops a moist coating as it enters the rim of the *Routhouni*. It is said that the people here are a bit snotty, tough around the edges but soft at the core."

"Ha! Is funny boy!" the driver exclaimed.

Cass gestured grandly out the window. "Exotic giant black hairs, waving upward from the ground and dotted with festive greenish globs, greet visiting tourists as they plunge upward into the—"

64

"Ew, Cass—just *ew!*" Aly said. "Can we leave him by the side of the road?"

On the outskirts of town, goats roamed in vast, sparse fields. Old men in ragged coats stared at us, their backs bent and their hands clinging to gnarled wooden canes. Black-clad old ladies sat knitting in front of rickety shacks, and a donkey ignored our driver's horn, just staring at us in the middle of the street. I felt strangely paranoid. I clutched the backpack tightly.

As we drove slowly through a flock of squawking chickens, I read the English section of a big, multilingual road sign:

You are aproching Routhouni the Prid of the Peloponnese!!!

"Prid?" Cass said.

"I think they mean 'pride,'" Aly answered.

Where on earth *were* we?

"Maybe we should have brought Dad along," I said. "This is pretty remote."

"We want the Massa to think we're alone," Aly said. "That was the plan. If we need to, we can call him."

I nodded. Dad had promised to hire a chopper if necessary, if anything were to go wrong. Which seemed weird, considering that "going right" meant being captured.

I tried to imagine Brother Dimitrios and his gang actually traveling to this place. I couldn't imagine *anyone* in his right mind traveling here.

We rounded a bend, following a narrow alley lined with whitewashed buildings. The car began swerving around potholes, bouncing like crazy. "Who paved this road," Aly grumbled, "Plato?"

"Is funny girl!" the driver barked.

He slowed to ten kilometers an hour as we crept toward the town center. I knew we were getting close by the sound of Greek music and the smell of fried food. Soon the dark, tiny street opened up into a big cobblestoned circular plaza surrounded by storefronts. We paid the driver and got out. I don't know what they were cooking, but I had to swallow back a mouthful of drool.

Did I say I was starving?

I was starving. I hadn't eaten in five hours.

Most of the shops were shuttering for the evening, but the cafés and restaurants were jumping. People strolled across the plaza, slowly and aimlessly, arm in arm. Kids chased each other and played catch. In the restaurants, stray cats wove around people's legs, looking for scraps, while entertainers in flowing costumes sang and played tambourines, guitars, and strange instruments that sounded like oboes. Old men sat silently outside the cafés at backgammon tables, sipping coffee and amber-colored drinks. An outdoor bar called America!! had two huge flat-screen TVs, one blaring a soccer game in Greek and the other an old rerun of *Everybody Loves Raymond* in English.

In the center was Zeus.

Or something Zeus-ish.

The statue glowered over the surroundings like a creepy, unwanted party guest. No one seemed to be paying it much notice. Its face and shoulders were peeling and pockmarked, like it had a skin disease. Its eyes were pointed in the direction of a flat-screen TV. Over time the eyeballs had eroded, so it looked like a grown-up Child of the Corn. In its raised hand was a big soccer ball–like thing, but I could barely see it under a dense crowd of birds.

"Behold, the Loculus of Pigeon Droppings," Cass mumbled, as we slowly walked around the plaza. "Held aloft by Zeus, God of Couch Potatoes, now approaching his record two millionth consecutive hour of TV viewing."

"Can't you be serious for once?" Aly hissed.

I could feel the curious eyes of the café-dwelling old men. One of the musicians moved toward us through the crowd—a girl about our age, maybe a little older. The hem of her skirt was raggedy, but the fabric was a rich patchwork of reds, purples, and blues, spangled with bright baubles. Her ankles and wrists jangled with bracelets. As she caught my eye, she smiled and then said, *"Deutsch? Svenska? Eenglees?"*

"Uh, English," I said. "American. No money. Sorry."

One of the café waiters came running toward us, shouting at the beggar girl to chase her away. As she ran off, he gestured toward the café. "Come! Eat! Fish! Music! I give you good price!"

Now customers and coffee sippers were staring at the commotion. "This is bad," I whispered. "We don't want to attract public attention. This is not how you stage an abduction. Kidnappers need quiet."

"Don't look now," Cass said, "but they're here. Other side of the plaza. We're six o'clock, they're twelve. Just to the left of the big TV!"

The TV was no longer playing *Everybody Loves Raymond* but an old black-and-white episode of *I Love Lucy.* Sitting at a small round table were four men in brown monk robes.

The Massarene.

I couldn't tell if they were the exact same goons who'd tried to kill us in Rhodes. We were too far away. Those pious robes hid a gang of thugs who would shoot at thirteen-year-old kids from helicopters.

"What do we do?" Aly asked.

"They tried to murder us once already!" Cass said.

"That was before the Massa knew who we were," I said. "Remember, they need us."

"So we just walk up to their tables?" Cass asked. "Like,

'*Yia sou*, dudes! Can we offer you some baklava for dessert, or maybe a kidnapping?'"

"Just let them see us," I said. "Come on, follow me."

The shortest route was directly across the plaza. People crisscrossed back and forth in front of us, as the sitcom's laugh track washed over the town square. The monks were eating and talking quietly, ignoring the TV. As we passed the statue, one of them looked up toward us. He had a thick brown unibrow and an intense, angry stare.

Aly tugged at my arm. "Where's Cass?"

I whirled around. I could see Cass a few feet behind us, at the base of the statue. He was helping up a crying little boy who had fallen on the cobblestones. The kid's parents smiled and thanked him, jabbering away in Greek. Cass backed away and tripped over a stone, too, landing against the statue. It looked like he was doing it on purpose, to cheer up the little boy and make him laugh. "I'll get him," I said.

But as I stepped toward Cass, I heard an odd cracking noise, like the turning of an ancient mill wheel.

The little boy shrieked, jumping into his father's arms. I could hear chairs scraping behind us, people screaming.

Pop! A jagged projectile of broken stone flew toward me and I ducked.

Pop! Pop! Pop! They were flying all around now.

I scrambled backward toward the café. The monks had

69

left their seats and were backing away. Desserts and dinners lay abandoned on tables, dropped to the ground.

"Jack!" Cass screamed.

High above him, the statue of Zeus turned, shedding more marble pieces. And it reared back with its staff, pointing it toward Cass.

CHAPTER TWELVE

BIIIIG TROUBLE

"CASS, GET AWAY from it—it thinks you're trying to steal the Loculus!" Aly screamed.

She dived toward Cass, pulling him away from the statue.

Zeus was moving by centimeters. Each jerk of his arm cracked the marble that encased him. "Lll . . . oc . . . ul . . . ssss . . ."

The word was just barely recognizable. Each syllable was accompanied by a sickening creak.

"Um . . . um . . ." I crawled backward. My tongue felt like a strip of Velcro.

I heard a chaos of noise behind us. Screams. Chairs clattering to the pavement. Children crying. The square was

71

clearing out. Aly clutched my left arm, Cass my right.

Within minutes, the square had completely emptied. No more old men. No bumbling waiters. No begging gypsies or bouzouki-playing musicians. Just us, the sound of the TVs, and the deep groans of the marble cracking.

A mist swirled up from the ground now in tendrils of green, yellow, and blue. It gathered around the statue, whistling and screaming.

The statue's expression was rock stiff, but its eyes seemed to brighten and flare. With a pop of breaking stone, its mouth shot open, and it roared with a sound that seemed part voice, part earthquake. The swirls sped and thickened, and in moments Zeus was juddering as if he had been electrocuted by one of his own thunderbolts.

In that moment we could have run.

But we stayed there, bolted to the spot by shock, as a bright golden-white globe landed on the stones with barely a sound and rolled toward a café. Its surface glowed with an energy that seemed to have dissolved the centuries of grit and bird droppings. I felt my body thrumming deeply, as if each artery and vein had been plucked like a cello.

"The Song of the Heptakiklos . . ." I said.

"So it *is* a Loculus!" Aly said.

I couldn't take my eyes from the orb. I staggered toward it, my head throbbing. All thoughts were gone except one: *If we could take this and then rescue the Loculus* of Health, we would have four.

"Jack, what are you doing?" Cass screamed.

I felt Aly grabbing me by the arm, pulling me away. We rammed into Cass, who was frozen in place, staring at the statue. We all looked up. Before our eyes, the statue's veins of marble turned blue and red, slowly assuming the warm, fluid texture of human skin.

Zeus was shrinking. The massive statue was becoming a man.

Or maybe a god.

As the mist receded, Zeus lowered his head. His eyes were a deep brown now, his face dark, and his hair iron gray. The muscles in his arms rippled as he stepped toward us, lifting the staff high above his head. *"Loculusss . . ."* he murmured.

"Give it to him!" Cass screamed. "He doesn't see it! He thinks you stole it! *Yo! Zeus! Your godliness! O Zeus! Look— it's on the ground!"*

"He doesn't understand English!" Aly said.

"IIII'LL GUB YOUUUU, MY PITY!" the statue bellowed.

"That sounds like English!" Cass said. "What's he saying?"

"Wait. 'I'll get you, my pretty'?" Aly said. "From *The Wizard of Oz*?"

The statue was moving slowly, creakily. It clearly hadn't

moved in a long time and its eyesight wasn't good. I had no intention of backing away. I wanted that Loculus. "Guys, I'm going after it. Back me up. Distract Zeus."

"Are you out of your mind?" Cass screamed. "We came here to be kidnapped!"

"We came here to win back our lives," I said. "Who knows if we'll ever have this chance again? *Back me up!*"

"B-but—" Cass stammered.

Aly placed a hand on his shoulder. Stepping between Cass and the statue, she straightened herself to full height. "Yo! Lightning Boy!"

The statue turned to face her.

And I moved slowly, step by step backward, through the shadows, toward the Loculus. The statue's eyes didn't waver from Aly. He was speaking a string of words in a strange language. It sounded vaguely Greek, of which I understand exactly zero, but the rhythms of it seemed weirdly familiar. Like I could hear the music but couldn't identify the instruments.

Go, McKinley. Now.

I turned. The pale moonlight picked up the contour of the fallen orb in the shadow of a café. As I crept closer, my head was jammed up with the Song of the Heptakiklos now. Gone was the noise from the TVs, from Aly's conversation. The Loculus was calling to me as if it were alive. As I reached for it, I heard something behind me, in a deep, growly rasp.

"OHHHH, LUUUUCY, YOU ARE IN BIIIIG TROU-BLE NOW."

I turned. Aly and Cass were both gawking at the statue. "Could you repeat that?" Aly said.

The statue lifted one leg and hauled it forward. It thumped to the ground. *"TO THE MOOOON, ALIIICE!"*

"What's he saying?" Cass asked.

"I Love Lucy," Aly said. *"The Honeymooners.* Those—those are lines from old sitcoms."

From behind me came the sound of a laugh track. "That TV . . ." I said. "Zeus has been watching it for years. Decades. It's the only English he knows. The sitcoms and the ads."

The former statue was staring at me now. Its pupils were dark black pools. The muscles in its face seemed to be tightening, its mouth drawing back. As I grabbed the Loculus, I felt a jolt up my arm, as if I'd stuck my finger in an electric socket. I tried to hold back a scream, gritting my teeth as hard as I could.

"Jack!" Aly screamed.

I turned just in time to feel a whoosh against my cheek. Zeus's staff flew past me, embedding itself in the ground.

Holding tight to the Loculus, I ran for the edge of the town square. In a moment Aly and Cass were by my side. "Follow me!" Cass shouted, leading us down an unlit alley-way.

As we raced out of town, I could see pairs of eyes staring at us out of darkened windows. Mothers and fathers. Children.

A voice behind us thundered loudly, echoing against the stucco walls. *"LOOOOCUULUUUUS!"*

CHAPTER THIRTEEN

The Fourth Loculus

IF I THOUGHT Zeus was a creaky old has-been, I was dead wrong.

We were running so fast I could barely feel my feet touch the cobblestones. But I could hear the steady thump of leather sandals behind us. The street was ridiculously narrow. We were running single file, with me at the rear, Aly in the middle and looking over her shoulders, and Cass in front.

"COWABUNGAAAA!" the statue shouted.

Aly's eyes widened. *"Duck!"* she cried.

I hit the ground. And Zeus's staff hurtled past us overhead like a javelin, impaling itself in the grate of a steel sewer basin with a metallic clunk.

I leaped to my feet, holding the Loculus under my arm like a football. Zeus wasn't more than twenty yards away now. I was going to be shish kebab unless I got the staff before Zeus did.

I scrambled and slid to a stop at the staff. Zeus roared when he saw what I was trying to do. The weapon was pretty well jammed into the grating, but on the third tug, I managed to pry it loose—along with the sewer grating, which went flying across the sidewalk.

"GGEEEEAAAAAGGHHH!" I didn't recognize the sound of my own voice. I lifted my arm and felt the weight of the staff. The thing must have been nearly as heavy as I was, but it felt impossibly light in my hands.

Zeus leaped toward me, arms outstretched. My body moved into action. I spun to the left. My arm swung the staff, connecting with the statue's legs in midair. He flipped forward, his face smacking hard onto the street. Without missing a beat, I raised the staff high and stood over him.

He rolled over and scrambled away on his back, a look of terror spreading across his face.

I could see Cass and Aly now, looking at me from behind the building in astonishment.

I was pretty scared, too. What had I just done?

"I WOULD HAVE GOTTEN AWAY WITH IT, TOO . . ." the statue said, *". . . IF IT WEREN'T FOR YOU MEDDLING KIDS . . . !"*

"What?" I replied.

*"I THINK THIS IS THE BEGINNING OF A BEAU-
TIFUL FRIENDSHIP."*

"Scooby-Doo!" Aly shouted. *"Casablanca!"*

"Is that his only English?" I said. "Aly, you're an old
movie geek. Can you give him an answer he'll understand?"

"Um . . . 'Surrender, Dorothy'?" she said.

But Zeus wasn't listening. Cocking his head, he stepped
forward, staring at me. I raised the staff, and he stopped.
"Masssarrrymmm?"

His voice was softer now. It was a question. A real question. And in a flash I was beginning to understand this
thing. "Wow . . ." I said. "He thinks I'm Massarym. He
thinks I'm the one who gave him the Loculus."

"M-m-must be a family resemblance," Cass said.

I stepped forward. "Jack," I said, pointing to myself. "I
am Jack."

"Dzack," the statue said, pointing to me.

"Right—Jack, not Massarym," I said. "So. Can't you
leave us alone? *Go back!* You don't need this Loculus. What
are you going to do with it? You're *Zeus!* You can throw
thunderbolts and stuff. Do you understand? *Go back!"*

Zeus shook his head. His cheeks seemed to sag.
"GO . . . ?"

"Home!" I said.

"PHONE HOME . . . ?" Zeus growled.

Oh, great. *E.T.* He was stomping closer to me now. That was the only way to describe it. His legs were muscular but still a little stiff. I could see now that his eyes were not a solid color but a roiling mass of shapes and colors, all tumbling around like a miniature storm. I backed off, keeping Cass and Aly behind me. With one hand I held tight to the Loculus, with the other I kept the staff firmly pointed.

"Just give it to him or he'll kill us!" Cass said, grabbing the Loculus out of my hands.

He caught me by surprise. As the Loculus came free, the staff fell from my grip. It was too heavy for me to hold. With a crack, it broke into three pieces against the cobblestones.

And in that moment, I knew exactly what kind of Loculus we had. Lifting that staff, leaping like a ninja—it wasn't adrenaline that let me do those things.

"Cass, that's a Loculus of Strength!" I cried out. *"Give it back to me!"*

Zeus and I moved toward him at the same time. With a scream, Cass jumped back and dropped the Loculus like it was hot. It rolled away down the street and I dived after it, landing with a thud on the sidewalk. As I hit the side of a building, I saw the Loculus resting against the bottom of a rain gutter opening a few feet away.

As I closed both hands around it tightly, I turned.

Zeus was coming at me now. In his hand was a dagger.

Its hilt was huge, its blade jagged like the edge of a broken glass bottle.

I heard Aly and Cass screaming. But I had the Loculus, and it gave me a power I never thought possible. I felt my free arm swinging downward, picking up a broken section of Zeus's staff.

I whirled, swinging the shaft like a bat. It connected with Zeus's torso and sent him flying across the narrow alley. As he hit the wall and sank down, I grabbed him by the collar and lifted him above my head.

I, Jack McKinley, had Zeus in the palms of my hands!

A thick, rusty nail jutted from the outer wall of a stucco building. I thrust Zeus against it, taking care that the nail ripped only through his thick tunic, not him. Because that's the kind of guy I am. At least when I have a Loculus of Strength.

Zeus roared, flailing wildly as he dangled from the wall. I knew he wouldn't stay up there long.

At the end of the alley were a couple of abandoned pushcarts. One of them was full of leather goods—satchels, sandals, sacks, clothing.

I ran over and grabbed an extra-large vest. Tucking the Loculus under my arm, I ripped a long shred of leather as if it were paper. "Stay calm," I said, approaching Zeus with caution. "This isn't going to hurt."

I grabbed his arms. I couldn't believe I was actually

wrestling them into position. As I tied them together tightly, Zeus cried out, *"I'LL GET YOU, YOU SKWEWY WABBIT!"*

As I backed away, Aly was laughing.

"What's so funny?" Cass said. "Did you see what Jack just did?"

"Sorry . . . sorry," Aly said. "It's just . . . Elmer Fudd?"

"Yeah, well, he doesn't look so godlike," I said, "but he'll break loose. Trust me, he's not going to stop until he gets his Loculus back. And I don't want us to be near him when that happens." I glanced over my shoulder. In the moonlight, the steep foothills of the Peloponnesian mountains looked to be about a mile or so away. They were dotted with trees and small black holes.

Caves.

"Let's book," I said.

We ran up the alley and wound through the streets away from the center of town, leaving Zeus's anguished cries behind.

Just behind a shack at the edge of town, I stopped. "Wait a second."

"Jack, we have to keep moving," Cass said. "We can't stay here. That thing is going to get loose and kill us."

"He turned into Zeus because we got close to him—we activated him," I said. "The same way that the other Select did, centuries ago. I'm hoping he goes back to being a statue once we're far enough away."

"Yeah, but he *killed* that guy, like, centuries ago," Cass said. "What if he doesn't turn back into a statue until he gets the Loculus back—and *then* kills us?"

"I say we call your dad," Aly suggested. "He can get us out of here. This was a bad choice. We need to put an ocean between us and him."

I thought a moment. Leaving Routhouni now, when I knew the Massa had spotted us, didn't seem like the best idea. We didn't have time before one of us had another episode and we used up the last of the shard. "We'll hide for a while up in the mountains," I said. "That way, if Zeus escapes, we'll see him coming. There's a chance the Massa will come after us there; you know they're going to want to get this Loculus. But at least we'll be safe. For a little while."

"If Zeus comes after us, we're going to need more than the Loculus of Strength," Cass said.

"I'll text Dad on the way," I said. "Maybe he'll have some ideas."

We turned and ran, leaving Zeus hanging.

CHAPTER FOURTEEN

ESCAPE FROM THE NOSTRIL

I MANAGED TO strap my flashlight to my head by making a kind of cap with leather strips. Holding the Loculus in one hand, I used the other hand to scrabble up the side of a rocky cliff. The Loculus was making this as easy as walking.

By the time I reached the first broad ledge, Cass and Aly were way behind me. "Show-off," Cass called up. His flashlight beam surfed up and down the scrubby mountainside.

"Take your time, mortals," I said.

I sat, unhooked my pack, and took a look at the text Dad sent me as we were leaving Routhouni. Just as I figured, he did have some ideas about what we should do:

Not keen on your plan. Am airlifting a package to you by chopper. Hoping you will regain your senses and return to the airport, fast and unseen. If not, what's in the bag should give you a fighting chance. Keep your GPS on. Never thought I'd say this, but hope the Massa find you soon.

I didn't know what was in the package. I hadn't had time to ask. But already I heard an engine roar overhead.

From the direction of the airport came a helicopter. I stood, waving. As it hovered overhead, a bay opened in its keel. A sack, tied to the end of a sturdy rope, lowered toward me.

He was sending us the Loculi!

"Honey, we're home," Aly announced, her arm appearing over the rim of the ledge.

I reached down and hauled her into the air and onto the ledge with one hand—as if I were lifting a rag doll. She sprawled in the dust.

"Curb your enthusiasm, Superboy," she said.

"Sorry, I'll try a different method." I sat on the ledge, dangling my legs just over Cass's head. "Grab on!"

"What?" Cass said.

"My ankle," I said. "Go ahead."

When I felt his hand clutching my ankle, I rolled onto my back. Curling my legs upward, I lifted Cass high. With a scream, he sailed clear over my head and came down onto the ledge near Aly. "Welcome," I said. "You're just in time for Santa."

Cass dusted himself off and looked upward. "What the—? Why is your dad giving us those?"

The sack was just over our heads now. I reached up and untied it. "He thinks that we're going to change our minds. Like, we'll take one look at the Loculi and say, 'Hey, let's go invisible and fly back to the airport!'"

"Actually, not a bad idea," Cass said.

"We're going to stay put and wait," I said.

We untied the rope and then I gave it a sharp tug, to indicate we were done. The rope rose back up into the bay. In moments, the helicopter was disappearing into the night, toward Kalamata.

Dad had attached a handwritten note to the sack: *Good luck and hurry back!*

I quickly stuffed the note into my pocket and shone the flashlight around the ledge. Behind me, in the mountain face, was a cave about four feet high. It was empty, its rear wall maybe twenty feet deep and covered with Greek graffiti. "If we need to, we can hide the Loculi in here," I said. "I'll try to text Dad to pick them up, after the Massa find

86

us. I wish he hadn't sent those things to us."

Aly was scanning the countryside. Routhouni was a distant cluster of dim lights in the darkness. The only other building between here and there was a tiny white house with a cross on its roof, in a field farther down the base of the mountains. "I don't see any headlights yet," I said.

"Do monks drive?" Cass asked.

"Of course they drive!" Aly said. "How else would they travel?"

"Sandals?" Cass said. "Camels? I don't know. We're just sitting ducks here."

I wanted to face the Massa. I wanted that badly. I don't know if it was the Loculus of Strength, or just the incredible rush of feeling that the hunt for the Seven Loculi was still alive. "We can't count on the Massa following us," I said. "Let's wait out the night here. If nothing happens, then we can get back to Routhouni in the daylight."

Cass was pacing now, squinting into the distance. "What about the lightning?" he said.

"What lightning? It's a clear night," Aly pointed out.

"He's *Zeus*, right?" Cass said. "What if he throws lightning bolts at us?"

"Zeus is mythological," I said.

"Oh, *that's* a relief!" Cass shot back. "I mean, whew, myths aren't real. That's as ridiculous as, like, I don't know . . . statues coming to life!"

"Easy, Cass," I said.

"He has a point," Aly piped up. "We're in the middle of nowhere. We saw a bunch of monks and we're assuming they're the Massa. Maybe the real Massa know enough not to be anywhere near this place."

Cass threw up his hands. "Yeah, well, maybe this whole thing was just a dumb idea."

"Whoa, what happened to our team?" I said. "We came up with this idea together. We can't just give it up. Not only that, we found another Loculus—so the way I see it, we're one step ahead. Plus, I just saved our lives and hung Zeus on a nail, and no one even said thanks. You guys want to call my dad and be picked up? Fine. But I'm going to finish this quest or die trying. I'll do what we're supposed to do, by myself."

I walked to the far end of the ledge and leaned against the rock face. I could hear Aly and Cass mumbling to each other. As far as I was concerned, I'd go back to the island alone. I had nothing to lose.

After a quiet moment I felt a hand on my shoulder. "Hey," Aly said.

"I don't know what's bothering you, Aly," I said. "You and Cass."

She was silent for a long moment. "When I came so close to death, Jack, it changed me. I'm not as afraid of it anymore, I guess. Part of me just wants to go home and be with Mom and my friends."

"I don't want you to die," I said. "Or Cass. Or me. Fourteen is too early."

Aly nodded. "Yeah. I think you're right. Thank you for nailing Zeus, Jack. You came through for us. I guess what I'm trying to say is, we are in this together. To the end."

"Bad choice of words," I said.

Aly laughed. "Sorry."

We sat, dangling our legs over the cliff. Cass joined us, leaning his head against Aly's shoulder. "I'm tired. And don't say, 'Hi, Tired. I'm Jack.'"

"I'm tired, too," Aly said. "We're twins."

"You guys get some sleep," I said. "I'll keep a lookout."

"How do we know you won't sleep, too?" Aly asked.

I grabbed the Loculus. "Popeye had spinach. Superman had the power of Krypton. I, Jack, have the Loculus of Strength."

Cass's eyes fluttered shut. A few seconds later, Aly's did, too. I was worried about both of them. I wasn't Popeye and I wasn't Superman. I needed them both, and I could feel them pulling away.

Overhead another military plane zoomed by, but neither of them stirred. I held tight to the Loculus and cast a wide glance over the barren countryside from left to right and back again.

And again.

By the fourth time, my eyes were heavy, too. There would be no fifth time until daybreak.

The "Strength" in the Loculus of Strength did not include staying awake.

CHAPTER FIFTEEN

THE DREAM CONTINUED

HE HAS FOUND me.

Again.

I thought I'd lost him in Halicarnassus. But here he is in Olympia, standing before me in the shop. Standing before a great, massive lump of marble that has traveled here by the work of twenty slaves over three months.

He has that look in his eyes. The Betrayed Commander. The look that caused troops to quake in their sandals. The look that made me cry when I was a coddled little princeling. But now, after all I've been through—after all my land has been through—he annoys me.

"You would do this to your own flesh and blood, Massarym?" are his first words. "This trickery? This disloyalty?"

I look deeply into his gray, stern eyes, trying to find the man I once adored and respected. "I would ask the same of you," I say. "As the king, your people are as your own flesh and blood. And you have allowed them to die. The ultimate disloyalty."

"The queen is at fault," he shouts, "and you, ungrateful wretch—"

"You cast a blind eye to Mother's actions then—but now you protest," I say. "You did not protest while she disturbed the balance of Atlantean energy. While she dissected and analyzed the power like some curious experiment. When she trapped it away from the earth itself into seven spheres—"

"Stealing those spheres is what caused the destruction!" he bellows. "Playing with them! Showing off!"

I am tired of this argument. I have work to do.

"Of that last part I am indeed guilty," I say. "But I realized early on that I was wrong. I returned them. If you are correct, everything should have been perfect again. Was it?"

The king is silent.

"Why the earthquakes, my king?" I say. "Why the monsters?" He turns away.

"Mother's actions—not mine—depleted the energy," I say. "She doomed Atlantis. Had we left the Loculi in place, they would have sunk away with the rest of the continent. Only by taking them and making them safe—stealing, as you say—could we have any hope for rebuilding. Minds of the future, minds greater than ours, will figure out what to do. I am not seeking

glory; I am not foolish. I want to house the Loculi for future generations, in the most magnificent forms imaginable." I gesture toward the block of marble. "Behold Zeus, Father! Does he not look like a living man?"

It looks nothing like a man. One can discern only the back of a giant throne—and the outline of what will one day become, according to plan, a likeness of the mighty god. The architects would have liked Zeus to be standing tall, but no temple could have been built high enough to do justice to this vision. So he will sit on a regal throne, his feet planted firmly. His staff has been separately sculpted, and it leans against the marble block. By its side is the Loculus of Strength.

It is this I want my father to see.

The lines of his face deepen, his eyes hollow. I have been waiting for this moment. In my time since leaving Atlantis, I have marshaled my own powers.

IMMOBILITUS.

My father is rooted to the spot. He tries to move toward the Loculus but cannot. "I will not allow this," he bellows. "I command you to return that to me!"

"I am not your soldier," I say.

"You are my son!" he replies.

I must fight a desperate pang of guilt. Shall I show mercy? His words tug at my heart.

But the deaths of thousands of Atlanteans tug harder.

I have much work to do. Structures to build. And I will not

be stopped. Not by any army. Not by Uhla'ar.

"You wish for your hands to be around that Loculus, rather than Zeus's?"

"Immediately!" he thunders.

"Then your wish, my father, shall be granted," I say. "Now and forever."

I feel the power welling up from my toes, spreading through my body like an intruder. It hurts. It blinds. I raise my hand toward my father, and I feel a jolt as if a hundred knives course through my veins.

Father's mouth drops open. His feet leave the ground, and he floats.

He is in midair now, screaming. I have never heard the king scream before. I know it is the last time I will ever see him.

But I turn away. I have already mourned the loss of my father. The loss of my people. My family now is the future. The people of the world yet unborn.

I walk away, forcing my ears to hear nothing.

CHAPTER SIXTEEN

A GOAT MOMENT

MY EYES FLICKERED open. I tried to hold on to the dream, but it was fading. I wanted to remember the details, to trap them in my brain, because they always seemed to mean *something*.

Already, in early versions of the dream, I'd seen Atlantis destroyed and the Loculi stolen away. Back then, it was as if I'd been trapped in the body of Prince Karai. But in these latest dreams, I'd been Massarym.

Somehow, being Massarym felt a whole lot worse.

"Hey," Aly said softly. "Are you okay?"

I sat up. The images were drifting away like smoke. I was on the ledge outside Routhouni. It was still dark. Middle of the night. Aly lay next to me on the ground, and

Cass was curled up into a fetal position behind us. I blinked myself deeper into reality.

"I wanted to kill him..." I mumbled. "Not me. Massarym."

"You wanted to kill Massarym?" Aly asked.

"No! *I* was Massarym," I said. "In my dream. I wanted to kill my father. The king of Atlantis, Uhla'ar. It was the second time I dreamed about him. The first was back when you were getting sick. I was Massarym then, too. Back then, the king was mad at me for stealing the Loculi. I threw a fake Loculus over the cliff in Halicarnassus. To fool him. This time we were near the Statue of Zeus. But it wasn't a statue yet."

The details were growing faint. Aly put an arm around my shoulder. "I have nightmares, too, but they're not like *that*. Shhh, it's okay."

"Yeah. Just a dream." Her arm felt warm, and I let my head touch her shoulder. In the distance, the lights of Routhouni flickered faintly. "Is it almost morning? We're going to have to make our move."

I heard a dull thump from above us.

Cass's eyes flew open. He spun around, looking up the hillside. "Did you hear that?"

Aly and I stood. "What kind of animals live on Greek mountains?" Aly asked.

"Goats?" I said.

My flashlight was still strapped to my head. I shone it

upward just in time to see something small and sharp hur-
tling downward.

Cass fell back, almost to the ledge. "*OWW!* The goats
are throwing rocks!"

Another rock flew downward. And another. "I don't
think those are goats."

"Let's get in the cave," Cass said.

As Aly and Cass headed for the opening, I grabbed my
backpack and the Loculus of Strength. I meant to follow
them, but something happened when I tucked that thing
under my arm.

I didn't want to hide. I was angry. Someone was trying
to scare us. What if this was a trap, bandits trying to force
us into a cave, a place we couldn't escape? After all we'd
been through, no way was I going to let this happen. I held
tight to the Loculus and dug my foot into the mountain
wall.

"Jack?" called Aly from inside the cave. "Jack, what are
you doing?"

My fingers dug into the dirt wall like hooks. They were
both yelling at me from the cave opening, but I blocked it
out. My muscles felt like steel coils as I climbed the cliff-
side.

"*Woo-HOO!*" I couldn't help shouting. I mean, come
on. Jack McKinley, the last guy picked for any sports team.
The boy who collapsed after one push-up. The winner of

the Most Times Shoved to the Ground by Barry Reese Award five years running. Now my friends were in danger and I could do something about it. I was climbing with the ease of . . . a goat!

This felt awesome.

Concentrate.

I hauled myself upward, maybe fifty feet, and reached my fingers over the rim of the next ledge. Then I hoisted myself straight upward and managed a three-sixty somersault in midair. Well, maybe three-forty, because I landed on my back. It wasn't the Loculus of Perfect Coordination, I guess.

Still, it didn't hurt at all, and I sprang to my feet. I turned my head, training the flashlight beam right and left. This ledge was narrower but longer from side to side.

There.

Above me. A tiny movement. Black against the blackness.

"Hello?"

As I looked up the hill, an outstretched body leaped at me. It knocked me off-balance, spinning me around. I fell to the ground, dropping the Loculus.

As I rolled away, my flashlight slid off my head. I grabbed it, the leather strips dangling. "Who's there?" I shouted, shining the light into the blackness.

"Jack? Are you okay?" Aly yelled from below.

I felt a hand land heavily on my shoulder. Leaping away, I spun to face my attacker.

Two eyes glared at me as if they contained light sources of their own. They were silvery white and definitely not human. "What do you want?" I said.

"WHAT DO YOU GO-O-O-OT?" came the reply, as the massive figure of Zeus hurdled toward me.

CHAPTER SEVENTEEN

BATTLE ON THE MOUNT

IT FELT LIKE a cow had dropped out of the sky and landed on my chest. I couldn't breathe under the weight. Zeus's mouth was inches from my face, but I felt no warmth and smelled no breath. He had one hand on the Loculus and it took all my effort to keep hold of it myself.

As long as I had contact, I could match his strength. I twisted my body hard. I kicked. Finally I just reared back my head and butted him on the forehead.

It hurt like crazy. But I guess it didn't feel too great for him either. He roared with surprise. And I took that moment to curl my legs upward, between his body and mine, and push hard. He fell away.

Unfortunately, the Loculus fell the other way. I

scrambled to my knees, swinging the flashlight.

The god-statue stood before me, legs planted wide, the broken section of his staff in his right hand.

"We're coming!" came Aly's voice from below.

I swung the beam around, looking for the Loculus. Zeus saw it first. He dived like a shortstop, reaching with his arms. I threw myself into his path.

Big mistake. Without the Loculus, my body took the hit hard. I bounced away, but I'd managed to knock him slightly off-balance, too, and we both tumbled to the rim of the ledge.

The Loculus rolled out of reach. Zeus and I lunged toward it at the same time. I was closer and my finger grazed the surface. But all I did was knock it over the ledge.

As it disappeared, I cried out, "Catch!"

Zeus roared and came for me, his fingers reaching for my neck. I could see the tempest in his eyes. So I did the only thing I could.

I bit him on the shoulder.

His eyes bulged. His arm froze. I jumped to the rim and flung myself over, praying I wouldn't overshoot the lower ledge.

"Jack!"

Aly was climbing up from below, her body pressed against the mountainside. She had caught the orb and was clutching it to her. I tried to jump clear of her, but my foot clipped the Loculus, dislodging it from her grip. Cass, who was below her, jumped back down to the ledge to get out of my way.

I landed beside Cass. Aly landed on top of me. It hurt but we were basically unharmed.

"Where's the Loculus of Strength?" I said, leaping to my feet.

"At the bottom," Cass cried. "I saw it falling."

I glanced upward. Zeus was at the edge, scanning the area. I would need to get down there, fast. I unhooked my backpack and took out the sack with the two Loculi. "I'll fly down there," I said, carefully removing the Loculus of Flight. "You and Aly take the—"

"*GERONIMO!*"

Zeus had jumped off the top ledge and was diving straight for me like I was a pool on a hot summer day.

I left the ground. Zeus landed at the spot where I'd been. He reached toward me, swinging with the broken staff. I heard it crack against my ankle, and I winced. But I was aloft, hanging tight to the Loculus of Flight.

I fought back the pain. The Loculus dipped and rose crazily. I felt like a disoriented bat.

Don't let it throw you off. Control. Think.

As I took a deep breath, the Loculus leveled out. The sun must have just risen above horizon, because I could see the outline of Zeus now. He was on our ledge, staring at me open-mouthed with astonishment. Cass was nowhere to be seen, but Aly was lowering herself downward from the ledge.

Of course. She had to let go of the Loculus of Invisibility. She needed two hands. *"Jack! Cass fell!"* she called out.

I looked down quickly, but the base of the cliff was a black pit, angled away from the moonlight.

"Cass!" I called out. *"Caaasssss!"*

I swung around and flew straight downward, landing on the ground harder than I meant to. My ankle throbbed so bad I expected it to fall off. I pulled out my flashlight and shone it around. The bushes and trees were a scraggly, dusty green, like fake props in a movie.

It took me three sweeps of the light beam before I saw a wink of solid-colored fabric from beyond the thick copse at the base of the cliff. I kept the light trained on it as I limped through brambles, somehow managing to step into every small animal hole along the way.

Cass's body was twisted so that he was facing up, while his torso was nearly turned to the ground. I knelt by him, cupping my hand around his head. The backpack, with a telltale round bulge, was on the ground next to him. He hadn't even gotten the Loculus out. "Cass," I said. "Are you all right?"

His eyes blinked. He seemed to have trouble focusing on me. "Aside from the pine needles in my butt," he said, "I'm pretty comfy. Owwwwww . . ." Grimacing, he rolled into a fetal position—just as Aly let out a scream from above.

I felt my blood run cold.

"Grab . . . the Loculus . . . of Strength . . ." Cass said.

I followed his glance with my flashlight until I saw the Loculus of Strength resting about ten feet away on a small, flat bush. I ran to it, flicked off the light, and dumped it back into my pack. "Thanks, Cass."

Holding one Loculus under each arm—Strength and Flight—I shot upward. The statue was scrabbling down the mountainside, inches from Aly. "Hey, Zeus!" I called out.

He turned to face me, his gnarled fingers digging into the dirt.

I circled above him. His teeth shone in the moonlight, gritted with anger. With my hands full of Loculi, I would have to use my legs. "You'll get a kick out of this," I said.

Swooping down, I smashed my foot into his jaw. His grip slipped. As he tumbled down the mountainside, head over heels, pain shot up my leg and my vision went totally white.

"Jack!" Aly cried out.

I steadied myself and flew up toward her. She reached out, grabbing my arm. "Are you okay?" she said.

"I'm glad I have Strength," I replied, sailing down toward Cass. "But at the moment, I kind of wish I had Healing."

I dropped to the ground, taking care to land on my good leg. "Can you . . . move, Cass?" I asked, grimacing at the pain.

"Break dancing, no," Cass replied. "Running from a deranged killer god, yes. What about you? You don't look so good."

I sat next to him, my eyes scanning the horizon. "Where is he—Zeus?"

"It was a pretty bad fall," Cass said. "If he wasn't dead, he might be now."

"He's a god," Aly replied. "How can he be dead?"

"We have to book before he sees us." I glanced around and noticed the small white shack in the distance. There was a cross on the roof. A church. "There."

"Wait. I thought we were going to go back to where the monks are," Aly said.

"I thought the statue would turn back to stone," I said. "He hasn't. He's going to come after us. Those innocent kids and families and old people in Routhouni—you think none of them will be hurt?"

"But—" Aly said.

"We have three Loculi, Aly," I said. "The Massa will know this. Wherever we go now, they will follow. We can't put all those people at risk. So let's move on!"

I put the Loculi down, reached for my phone, and sent Dad a text:

> in trouble! come now.

> white church agnst mtns outside Routhouni.

"Vamanos," I said, standing up.

On the other side of the bush, a great black shadow rose like a wave from the sea. *"WHO YOU GONNA CALL?"*

A fist slammed against my chest and I fell backward.

Zeus crashed through the bush. I tried to stand but my ankle collapsed, shooting pain up the side of my body.

Through slitted eyes, I watched the god-statue sprint back toward town, the Loculus of Strength tucked under his arm, as another jet passed overhead.

CHAPTER EIGHTEEN
LOSER, LOSER, LOSER

on my way. u ok? what happened?

LIMPING TOWARD THE white church, I stared at the message from Dad.

My ankle felt like it had been twisted off and shoved back on again. Cass's shirt was in tatters, his face scarred by branches. Aly looked like an extra from *The Walking Dead*. Now that the sun was peeking up, I could see every painful detail of my friends' injuries.

Zeus was long gone. By now he'd probably turned back into a statue again. Maybe back in Routhouni, maybe on the way.

I didn't want to find out. There'd be time to battle him again later. "How do I begin to answer this message?" I muttered.

"How about: "Sup, Pop?' " Cass said. "'We tried to steal a Loculus from a god who learned English by watching TV sitcoms. Jack pinned him to a wall, but he came back and nearly killed us. How was your sleep?'"

"It's not only sitcoms," Aly said. "Movies, too. When Jack asked him what he wanted, he answered, 'What do you got?' That's a line from *The Wild One*. Marlon Brando, 1953."

Cass nodded. "For you, that counts as a new release."

I blocked them out and began typing out a message to Dad:

long story. c u at white church.

Shoving the phone into my pocket, I continued the trudge across the rocky terrain. No one said much. I tried to look on the positive side. We were alive. We had located a Loculus.

That was about it for the positive side.

Destroyed Loculus of Healing? Check.

Lost Loculus of Strength? Check.

Brought maniac god to life and possibly set him loose on innocent Greek townspeople? Check.

Didn't even come close to attracting Massa, which was the whole reason we got into this mess in the first place? Check.

We were a team of losers, alone in the dark in the middle of nowhere, without a clue.

Loser, loser, loser.

I took a deep breath. Professor Bhegad had had names for the four of us. *Soldier, Sailor, Tinker, Tailor.* Cass was the Sailor who always knew how to navigate. Aly was our geeky Tinker of all things electronic. We'd lost our Soldier, Marco the Great and Powerful, to the Massa.

As the Tailor, I was . . . well, nothing, really. *The one who puts it all together*, according to Bhegad. As far as I was concerned, that was his lame way of saying *none of the above*.

There was nothing inside me for the G7W gene to make awesome.

Looking at my bedraggled friends, I figured the least I could do was put on a good face. "Hey, cheer up," I said. "It ain't over till the fat lady sings."

"Loo-loo-loo-LOOOOO!" Cass crowed like a demented soprano.

I had to laugh. But my ankle buckled again and I stopped.

Aly knelt by my side, touching my leg gently. "Is it broken? Zeus hit you pretty hard."

"No, I don't think it's broken," I replied. Her touch did nothing for the pain, but I liked the way it felt. "He did hit it hard, though. If my leg were a baseball, it would have been over the center field wall."

"Let's rest," she said gently. "Oh. And, by the way—thanks, Jack."

"For what?" I said.

"For your bravery," she replied. "You really took one for the team."

My temperature shot up about ten degrees.

"Um, I don't want to spoil your magic moment, but we have to move." Cass fumbled around in his pocket and pulled out the shard of the Loculus of Healing. Squatting next to Aly, he wrapped his hand around my ankle, pressing the shard into my skin.

"No! Cass!" I cried, pulling my leg away. "Save it. Look, we've missed our chance with the Massa and we don't know when we'll see them again. Let's save the shard."

I stood and balanced my weight from leg to leg. It hurt, but I knew I could make it.

"You sure?" Aly said, and I nodded.

We began trudging to the church again. My ankle throbbed, but the pain seemed to get better the more I walked. "One thing—let's all promise to stay healthy from now on," I said. "So we don't use that thing up any faster than we have to."

Aly and Cass both grunted in agreement.

For all the good it will do us, I did not say.

* * *

Sleeping isn't easy when the saints are staring at you.

The little church had white stucco walls. In it were a few rows of pews, a small altar made of polished wood, and a hard marble floor.

Plus gigantic paintings in brilliant reds and golds that were so realistic it felt like you were being judged from all directions.

Somehow Cass and Aly had nodded off, but I was wired.

I looked at my watch. It had been nearly an hour since I'd texted Dad. Where was he?

Outside the sun had risen. The air was cool and crisp. I scanned the horizon but it was completely still.

Taking out my phone, I tapped out a quick message:

WHERE R U?

It didn't take long for the reply:

WHERE U?

Oh, great. For all I knew there were tons of these little churches and he was completely confused.

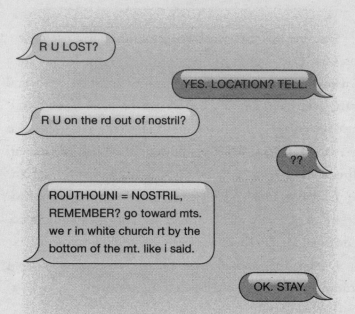

R U LOST?

YES. LOCATION? TELL.

R U on the rd out of nostril?

??

ROUTHOUNI = NOSTRIL, REMEMBER? go toward mts. we r in white church rt by the bottom of the mt. like i said.

OK. STAY.

I figured Dad was either panicked or driving. Or both. Those short texts were not his usual old-school style, with complete sentences. "Later, guys," I said to the saints as I headed outside to wait.

The moment I stepped out the door, I spotted a movement on the horizon. My pulse quickened. *"Here! Over here!"* I shouted.

Cass stumbled outside, yawning, his hair all bunched on one side. "I hope he's bringing breakfast."

Aly emerged behind him. Her purple hair hung at her shoulders, and her face seemed softer somehow. I smiled. "Good morning."

"What are you staring at?" she asked.

"Nothing." I turned away, gesturing out toward the horizon. "Dad's coming!"

Cass squinted into the distance, shielding his eyes against the sun. "Uh . . . did he grow a huge black beard since yesterday?"

I could see the shape of the car now. Dad had rented a Mercedes coupe at the airport, but this was a minivan jammed with people. The driver's window was down, and as the van got closer, I could make out a guy with gray hair, glasses, and a ZZ Top beard. He called out something in Greek, waving his arm.

"A priest," Aly said. "Oh, great, we're trespassers in a house of worship."

I didn't like the looks of these guys. But then again, I wasn't used to seeing Greek priests. *"Hello!"* I called back.

"No speaky Greeky!" Cass chimed in.

As the car pulled up to the church, the man smiled. I could see now that he was wearing a dark robe. "Americans?" he asked. "Early for the service?"

"Right!" Cass squeaked.

Now the back doors were opening. Two other men, all in long robes, climbed out of the minivan. It seemed like a lot of priests for such a little church.

And priests did not usually carry firearms.

"Jack . . ." Aly said, taking my arm.

My eye was on the person now emerging from the

passenger door. As he stood and walked toward us around the minivan, he smiled and held out his arms.

Cass and Aly stiffened.

"Good morning," said Brother Dimitrios. "I always had faith I would see you again."

CHAPTER NINETEEN

DEIFIRTEP

THE BACKPACK.

I still had it. We hadn't hidden it away.

Great. The plan was to be captured by the Massa, but not to give them the whole store!

Cass and Aly were both staring at the pack. It was too late to do anything about it now. "What did you do to my father?" I asked. "How did you get his cell phone?"

"Jack, whatever are you talking about?" Dimitrios said, laughing. "Your father is still with his plane. We don't need to steal a cell phone to find you."

He stepped forward, open arms, as if he wanted to give me a hug hello. But I knew enough about Dimitrios's friendliness. It was as fake as a plastic jack-o'-lantern.

I shrank away, out of his grip. "Come now, no need to be afraid. You should be delighted."

One of Dimitrios's goons was opening the back door of the minivan.

"So . . . we're supposed to go with you?" Cass squeaked.

"It's not uncomfortable," Dimitrios said. "We will drive smoothly."

"So, um, what are you going to do to us?" Cass blurted out.

Dimitrios chuckled. "Celebrate, of course. Over the triumphant news—that there is new hope for your lives!"

Cass and Aly eyed me warily. Neither of them moved.

"Children, let's be open," Dimitrios said. "The Massa, as you know, are all about openness. You are carrying two Loculi. And, if I'm correct, you also have the remaining pieces of the Loculus of Healing."

I gasped. *"How did you know?"*

"Because, dear boy, we could not find them in New York," Dimitrios said. "And we recovered everything. Think about it—with your pieces and ours, we may be able to resume the search for Loculi! We will have three! Look around. Do you see the Karai Institute coming after you to save your lives? No! But, voilà—here we are!"

"Who loves ya, babe?" grunted Dimitrios's helper, gesturing toward the back of the van.

Three. He hadn't said a thing about Zeus's Loculus.

"So . . . how did you know we were here?"

"We have spent years recruiting agents," Dimitrios replied. "Our man in this area drives a taxi. He found you very amusing."

"The taxi driver?" Cass said. "He was too nice to be a Massa."

Brother Dimitrios's smile faded. But all I could think about were the monks. They weren't Massarene after all. They were actual monks.

Which meant Dimitrios didn't know about Zeus or the fourth Loculus.

I took a deep breath and headed into the back of the minivan. Aly and Cass climbed in beside me, and the door shut with a loud thump. With a *shusssh* of tires in the dirt, the van turned and began heading back across the stubbly plain. *"Remind me why we're doing this,"* Cass hissed.

"To get to the island," I whispered back. "To reconstruct the Loculus of Healing. Remember? Our plan?"

"Were we out of our minds?" Cass said. "Did you see these guys? What if they kill us?"

"What are you going to do to us, Brother D?" Aly demanded.

"Are you afraid?" Dimitrios asked, turning to face us.

"Deifirtep," Cass said.

Dimitrios looked at him blankly for a moment, then burst into laughter. *"Petrified!* Oh, yes, I got that. What fun we'll have with your witty little habits! Well, you needn't be scared. You'll see. Now. I have a question for you. I confess your visit defies a certain logic. Do you fail to grasp the significance of what you did in New York City? Destroying the Loculus meant destroying yourselves."

"Yeah, we grasp it," Aly said. "Do you grasp that we saved your life? You'd be a zombie by now, wandering around in Bo'gloo, if we hadn't jumped in."

"Drooling," Cass added. "Really bad skin. No blood. You'd hate it."

Dimitrios blanched. "You are so right—how rude of me not to thank you. I was headed for the underworld. As was Sister Nancy. You acted bravely by destroying that Loculus and thus closing the gates."

Sister Nancy. As in Nancy Emelink. An anagram of Anne McKinley, aka my mom. How long would she be able to use that name? I worried about her. All those years we thought she was dead, she'd risen incognito to the top of the Massa—but now she seemed to want to help me. And I wanted to protect her secret. What would they do to her if they found out?

"You're welcome," I said. "And we do know we're as good as dead, if that's what you're asking."

"Not anymore," Brother Dimitrios said with a smile. "You will be happy that we are well along the way to assembling the pieces of the Mausoleum Loculus. Piece by piece.

Except for the sections you have. Which you will hand over now."

Dimitrios held out his palm toward me. I could feel Cass and Aly stiffen.

"No!" I blurted.

"No?" Dimitrios said. "That disappoints me. I would hate for someone to have to search you. We were just getting to be friends."

I quickly took out the shard and showed it to him.

"Jack!" Aly cried out.

"You're welcome to take this," I said, "but you don't want to."

I explained that the shard was keeping us alive. That if he took it away, one or all of us would go into a coma. "Of course, maybe that's what you want," I said. "For us all to die right here in your van. But it would be a shame to lose the only people who can find the other Loculi . . ."

Brother Dimitrios's fingers were millimeters from the shard. He raised an eyebrow high and sighed. "All right," he said. "But don't try anything rash. Like trying to escape. We need you and care about your lives dearly."

"Sir!" a voice called from the front of the van.

Dimitrios spun around. We were heading east, the sun rising in front of us, huge and swollen like an angry furnace. Where it met the pavement, a black dot shimmered as it slowly drew closer.

Dad.

I shoved the shard into my pocket, sneaked out my phone, and quickly typed out a text:

> PLAN WORKING! IN BLK MINIVAN W BROTHER D. GO AWAY. PLS DO NOT MEET US!!!!

Brother Dimitrios leaned forward. The dot on the horizon was growing larger by the second. It was a dark car, sending up clouds of dust behind it, traveling ridiculously fast. As the Massa driver veered to the left to avoid its path, the car veered with it.

I squinted against the glare of the sun as the car headed toward us.

A Mercedes coupe.

"No, no, no, no," I murmured. "Not now . . ."

Aly gripped my arm.

"What is that idiot doing?" Brother Dimitrios shouted, his eyes focused on the road ahead. "Shake him, Mustafa!"

"He's crazy!" the driver shouted back.

We lurched back and forth violently as Mustafa tried to avoid collision, but the Mercedes was bearing down on us. I had never seen Dad drive like this.

I felt myself falling to the floor in a tangle of limbs with Aly and Cass. Grabbing the back of the seat, I hoisted myself up enough to see a brief flash of blue metal through the windshield.

The sound of the collision exploded in my ears. I somersaulted forward, jamming against the minivan's backseat. The minivan spun twice, then came to a stop. As Brother Dimitrios pushed me away, I caught a glimpse through a side window.

Dad's car was upside down, its roof crushed in.

"Dad!" The scream ripped upward from my toes. I pushed open the rear door of the minivan and jumped out.

Outside, I could see one of the Massa slumped in the passenger seat of the minivan, groaning, clutching his bloody forehead. I limped past him toward Dad's car. It was about ten feet away. A plume of black smoke belched out from the hood, and the whole thing looked like it was about to blow, but I didn't care. I knelt by the passenger window, hoping to see him. *"Dad! Are you okay? Say something!"*

I was answered by a loud metallic *grrrrrrock!* from the other side of the car, accompanied by the tinkle of broken glass.

The driver's door.

I leaped to my feet in time to see a thatch of coppery red rising over the car's upended chassis.

"Something," said Torquin.

CHAPTER TWENTY

IN THE MATTER OF VICTOR RAFAEL QUIÑONES

I HAD NEVER been so unhappy to see the belching, bearded, barefoot giant in my life.

"What did you do to my father?" I screamed. "How did you get his car?"

"Stole car," he said, shrugging as he waddled past me, a black leather bag in one hand and a metal crowbar dangling from the other. "At airport. He was there. I was there. I needed car. He didn't." His small green eyes stared out from under the shelf of his blood-soaked forehead, intent on Brother Dimitrios.

"Ah, my good man . . ." Brother Dimitrios approached Torquin with a wary hand outstretched. "Surely we can discuss this like two civilized—*augh!*"

Torquin took his hand, lifted Dimitrios over his head, and tossed him to the ground like a sack of potatoes.

Two of the other priests were racing away, kicking up dust across the field, their sandals flying off in midair. "Come back!" Torquin bellowed after them, rearing back with the crowbar. "No fun!"

Torquin dropped the leather bag. With a couple of strangely delicate steps, he heaved the crowbar like a javelin. But my eyes were distracted by a glint of metal from the minivan. I heard a soft click.

Mustafa was leaning out the driver's window, taking aim at Torquin with a rifle.

I ran toward the shooter, screaming at the top of my lungs. Cass was way ahead of me. Directly in the gun's line of sight.

Brother Dimitrios sat up, his face taut with urgency. *"Don't hurt the boy!"* he shouted.

A *craaack* split the morning air. A puff of smoke.

Cass and Torquin dropped to the dirt. Aly was shrieking, taking off after them in a sprint.

I grabbed the passenger door handle and yanked it open. The driver swung his head to look at me, his eyes wide with shock. Before he could bring his arms back through his window, I rammed him with my head. Then I reached for the window button and squeezed as firmly as I could.

The window slowly rose, trapping the driver's arms. His

curses turned to screams as I switched off the ignition key, trapping the window in position. "Get the rifle!" I yelled.

Aly was already running toward Mustafa. She grabbed the rifle and yanked downward. With a cry of pain, Mustafa let go. The rifle went clattering to the dirt.

"Cass!" I shouted. "Torquin!"

My feet barely touched the ground as I ran toward the two bodies. Cass was struggling to sit up. "I'm okay," he said. "Torquin jumped into the path of the bullet. He fell against me."

We hunched over Red Beard. His face was covered in dirt and his eyes rolled upward. A trickle of blood ran from his mouth down the side of his cheek. Aly slapped his cheeks, screaming his name. *"Don't die! Torquin, you are not allowed to die!"*

"Arrrgh, why did he do this?" Cass said.

I reached into my pocket for the shard. It was so small. If we used it again, we risked losing it.

"Do it, Jack," Aly said.

I nodded. Torquin's bratwurst-sized fingers were twitching. I knelt next to him. I felt the shard growing warm in my palm.

I brought the shard carefully toward Torquin's chest. Cass leaned over the big man and said, "Hang in there, dude."

Before the shard made contact, Torquin shuddered and sat bolt upright. "Arrrmmgh . . ." he grunted.

Cass lurched away from him. "Auuu, Torquin, what did you eat for lunch? Dog food?"

What was left of the shard slipped from my palm, fell against Torquin's leg, and disappeared in the grass.

* * *

The Massa priest with the bloody forehead had made a run for it. Torquin was thirty yards away, dragging the other priest toward us by his clerical collar.

But my attention was focused on a patch of pebbles and scraggly grass. "Found it!" I cried out, closing my fingers around the shard.

It was the size of a pebble and nearly weightless. I could barely feel it in my hand. "What if we lose this?" Cass asked.

"We can't afford to," Aly said. "Put it in a supersafe place. Like, surgically, under your skin."

I did the next best thing. I tucked it into my wallet. It wouldn't get lost there.

"Alive," Torquin's voice rasped. He flopped the unconscious priest down in the dirt beside us. A welt the size of a small boulder was growing from the top of his head.

Proudly, Torquin held up the crowbar. "Set high school record for javelin."

"You threw that and actually hit him?" I asked.

"You went to high school?" Cass asked.

I looked around. The van driver and Brother Dimitrios were both as unconscious as the crowbar victim. "Okay, time out," I said. "This is all wrong. *So* wrong. But before we start yelling at you, Torquin, tell me what exactly happened with you and my dad."

"Said hello," Torquin said. "Asked if he wanted to come. He said no. Frustrating. Torquin asked to borrow phone when he went to bathroom. Took phone. And took car."

I took it with two fingers. "So those texts from Dad . . . were from you?"

Torquin nodded.

I lowered my voice. "Didn't he tell you—we're trying to be captured."

"Um . . ." Torquin said.

"Where have you been, Torquin?" Aly said. "You just disappeared on us in New York!"

"And is your name really Victor Rafael Quiñones?" Cass said.

Torquin took a deep breath. Then he belched.

"That is so gross," Aly said.

"Happens when Torquin is excited," Torquin said. "Hate the name Victor."

Cass laughed. "I hate my real name, too—Cassius!"

"Shakespeare," Torquin said. "From *Julius Caesar.* The 'lean and hungry look.'"

"I can't believe you know that," Cass said.

"Torquin with Omphalos now, head of Karai," Torquin barreled on. "Omphalos gave jet to Torquin. Slippy—nice jet." He pointed to the leather bag he'd dropped on the ground. "In case meet Massa, supposed to use meds . . . injections. Pah! Crowbar easier."

"So wait, you were here to get Brother Dimitrios?" Aly asked.

"No!" Torquin replied. "Orders to get you back. Meds just in case."

"Back to where?" Cass asked. "Where is the KI now?"

"Can't tell," Torquin replied.

"Who is the Omphalos?"

"Don't know," Torquin said.

I took Torquin aside, far from any potentially listening Massa ears, and explained our whole story—Aly's healing, the fused shard, the plan to let the Massa kidnap us. He listened carefully, grunting and frowning as if this were a crash course in advanced calculus.

As he looked over the unconscious Massa, his eyes welled up. "So Torquin made big mistake . . ."

"They'll wake up," Aly said. "We can salvage the plan."

"Professor Bhegad would be mad at Torquin!" The big man pounded his fist into his palm. "Missing Professor Bhegad. Very very m-m-much . . ."

Cass looked aghast. "You're not going to cry, are you? Maybe you've been reading too much Shakespeare?"

"We all miss him, Torquin," Aly said. "But before you get too upset, let's figure a way out of this."

127

"Come with us," Cass said.

"He just drove Dimitrios into the dust," Aly said.

Cass shrugged. "Maybe he can stow away? Or follow us with Slippy?"

"We can't let our plan fall apart," I said.

"No. Your lives most important." Torquin scrunched up his brow, looking at the unconscious Massa. He took a couple of locomotive breaths, like a bull. Closing his eyes, he held the crowbar high over his head. "Do it."

We looked at each other, baffled. "Uh, do what?" I said.

Beads of sweat had formed at the edges of Torquin's forestlike beard. "Before Massa wake up," he said, "you knock out Torquin."

CHAPTER TWENTY-ONE

SLIPPING AWAY

I WASN'T EXACTLY expecting Brother Dimitrios to break out into a Greek dance, but I thought he'd be happy to see Torquin flat out on the ground.

Instead he wiped his forehead with a handkerchief, shaking his head in disbelief. "I thought we'd already taken care of that ape."

If only he'd known how hard it had been to knock out Torquin. The guy's head was as hard as granite. So I, Jack McKinley, swung the crowbar like a cleanup hitter. With a loud *craaack*, I whupped him so hard upside the head that he flew through the air like a rag doll. My brave action caused Aly to swoon. She declared at the top of her lungs that Marco was a distant memory. Because of my own awesomeness.

I hope you don't believe that.

Truth was, I couldn't possibly hit Torquin. None of us had the stomach to do the dirty deed. He may have been crude and weird, but he'd been our friend and protector. Sort of. So we finally convinced him to use the meds in his black bag. One of them was a tranquilizer that got the job done in a few seconds. And out he went.

Dimitrios reached inside the minivan. "I suppose I should take care of him permanently," he grumbled.

"*No!*" we all shouted at the same time.

"Please," Aly said, "leave him alone and we promise we won't resist going with you."

"Torquin is harmless," I quickly added. "Now that the Karai Institute has been destroyed, he's just . . . deluded. Really. He's harmless."

Brother Dimitrios stood over the unconscious priest. "Doesn't look so harmless to me."

With a loud *whoosh*, flames began shooting up from the crashed rental car. It was maybe fifteen feet away from Torquin.

"I'd better not regret being merciful." Scowling, Brother Dimitrios grabbed the knocked-out priest and dragged him toward the minivan. "Let's get out of here, now," he called out.

"Wait, what about Torquin?" Aly asked.

But Dimitrios was already starting the engine and extracting Mustafa from the window. As he shoved Mustafa to the passenger side, he grabbed the rifle. *"Get in! Now!"*

Cass eyed Torquin. "He'll be okay, Jack. He can find his way back after he comes to. Come on, let's go."

We climbed into the minivan. With a screech of tires, the van swerved around Dad's rental car and peeled down the highway. I stared at Torquin's inert body, a receding black lump near the smoking car.

A moment later a deep boom shook the road, and the minivan's rear wheels rose off the ground. As we thumped down, Cass, Aly, and I pressed our faces against the van's rear window. My throat closed up.

Torquin's body was nowhere to be seen. A thick, fiery black cloud billowed from where he'd been lying.

* * *

Losing Torquin was like a knife to the gut.

"I can't believe this . . ." Aly murmured.

"I don't," Cass said, his face ashen. "I don't. He's alive. He escaped. He . . ."

Cass's voice trailed off. As the black cloud billowed, the acrid smoke reached us clear across the deserted plain. We must have been two miles away. Even the wildest wishful thinking wasn't going to bring him back.

"He saved our lives so many times . . ." Aly murmured.

In Egypt after an explosion, on the island during the Massa attack—time and time again he'd been there for us. I thought about the first time I'd met him. He'd caught me trying to escape the island and forced me back to Bhegad—even that may have saved my life.

We all owed him, big-time.

And we'd never be able to repay.

I fought back tears. Aly and Cass were slumped against one side of the van, holding hands tightly. "He didn't deserve that . . ." Cass said softly.

"I guess he's with P. Beg now," Aly replied, forcing a wan smile.

I nodded. "Bhegad's probably happy. He's got someone to scold."

Cass looked as if he'd aged three years. "It's my fault. I said he'd be all right. I said we should leave him there . . ."

"Cass, don't even think that," Aly said. She put an arm around him, but he was stiff as a plank.

"It's all our fault, Cass," I said. "We knocked him out."

"He *asked* us to," Cass said. "We never should have said yes. It was the dumbest thing we ever did."

The trip was slow, the Kalamata streets jammed with traffic. It was just after noon by the time the minivan pulled up to the private-terminal gate of the airport. I felt numb. My brain kept asking if there was something I could have done.

By now Mustafa was awake and groggy. A guard checked Dimitrios's papers but he seemed distracted by messages coming in through his headset. "Better hurry, sir," the guard said. "There's been some trouble at the military base and flights are limited."

We sped across the tarmac, past about a half dozen private aircraft. "Look," Aly whispered, pointing to a sleek jet that was being hosed down by a chain-link fence.

Slippy.

There was no mistaking the Karai stealth jet we'd flown in so many times. I wondered how long it would take the Omphalos—whoever that was—to realize the jet wasn't coming back.

I looked around for Dad. I had no idea where he was right now, but I half expected him to come running out.

Wherever you are, I thought, *don't worry. We'll be back.* Maybe if I repeated that enough times, I'd believe it myself.

The van came to an abrupt stop. "Move!" Brother Dimitrios shouted.

We emerged from the minivan and ran up a set of metal steps to a small black eight-seater jet. Dimitrios pushed me into a thick, comfortable seat by the window.

I watched Slippy shrink to the size of a toy as we headed out over the Mediterranean.

CHAPTER TWENTY-TWO

MASSA ISLAND

I DRIFTED IN and out of sleep. Dimitrios offered us lunch, but even though I hadn't eaten in a gajillion hours, I wasn't hungry. In my waking state, I couldn't shake the image of Torquin on the ground.

For about the hundredth time, I absentmindedly touched my pocket to make sure the small shard was still there. We couldn't lose that.

A flurry of Greek words filtered back to us from the front of the aircraft. Mustafa happened to be the pilot, and after what I'd done to him in the minivan, he was not a happy camper. If Dimitrios hadn't been there, I think he would have pounded me into hamburger by now.

"Seat belts!" Mustafa snapped.

We buckled ourselves in. The sky became thick with clouds, and sharp strips of lightning crackled all around us. The plane bucked and rolled. My shoulder slammed into the airplane wall. I heard a metallic *grrrrockkk* from the underside of the plane.

I vowed to stay calm. We'd been through this before. Strange weather always surrounded the island. These were signs the plane was getting close. "Did you ever think . . ." Aly said, bouncing left and right, "that the island has a mind of its own . . . and it doesn't like the Massa?"

"Maybe if you show your smiling face out the window, it'll know friends are arriving," I said.

Aly gripped my hand tightly. My stomach was fluttering. I should have hated the idea of returning to this sweltering, half-destroyed home of deadly creatures and horrible memories. But I was more excited than scared. "Can I confess something to you?" I said. "I hate this place but I feel a little . . . excited. Like, happy to be back. Tell me I'm not crazy."

"You're not crazy," she replied. "I feel it, too."

I braced myself, expecting her to talk about seeing Marco again. But she quickly added, "We actually have a chance to live now."

"True," I said.

"You know what else?" Aly added. "I sense Torquin is at our backs, cheering us on."

We looked at Cass, who hadn't said a word the whole flight. He was staring out the window as if tracking the flight of a ghost. Aly leaned forward and put a gentle hand on his shoulder. "Still thinking about the big guy, huh?"

Cass shifted away from her and exhaled without answering.

In truth, I wasn't thinking about our plan, or about Torquin. As Aly settled back, I said, "I'm nervous about seeing my mom again, Aly. I don't know how to feel about her."

"She slipped you that shard, Jack," Aly said. "She must be on our side."

I shook my head. "It doesn't add up. I mean, *no contact* for seven years? And then, boom, she shows up at Massa headquarters in Egypt—and she's like one of the heads of the whole organization?"

"Jack, she was the one who made it possible for you to escape that headquarters—with the Loculi!" Aly said.

"And look where we are now," I said. "Aly, what if she's fooling us—making us *think* she's a spy? This may all be a trick to get us over to the Dark Side." I took a deep breath and watched as the clouds began to clear and the plane to steady. "I don't trust my own mom. But I really, really want to see her again."

The island became a kidney-shaped green dot in the midst of a bright turquoise sea. Most of it was carpeted with a jungle of dense green, broken only by the solid black peak of Mount Onyx. Bright yellow beaches ringed the northern coast. Soon I could make out the orderly geometry of the Karai Institute campus—red-brick buildings surrounding a quadrangle crisscrossed with brick paths.

From a distance it looked as though the Massa attack had never occurred—the soldiers hunting us down, the fires and the bombings, the chases through the trees. But as we flew closer to the campus I saw uncut grass and weed-choked paths, blackened sections of buildings that had been bombed or torched. People in ragged white uniforms were dragging equipment into the buildings, guarded by others in black suits with rifles strapped across the backs. "Those must be KI prisoners," Cass muttered.

I looked over toward the jungle. With Torquin's help, a band of Karai had escaped there with our friend Fiddle. But my eyes fixed on three plumes of black smoke deep in the jungle. "I hope the rebels aren't in that . . ." I said.

"Or Marco . . ." Aly added.

Marco. There it was. I could see her eyes lighting up.

"Marco's one of the Massa," I reminded her. "Probably safe and well fed and shooting three-pointers from the top of Mount Onyx."

"That would be, like, three-thousand-pointers," Aly said.

The plane dipped its wings. Way down below, I could see black-suited guards waving at us. We dropped fast and touched down smoothly at the airport. This was where Fiddle would always greet us, his geeky ponytail swishing left and right as he eyeballed the jet for damage.

As the pilot pushed open the door, a severe-looking woman with the trace of a mustache stood at attention. "At your service, Brother Dimitrios!" she barked. "Welcome back to Massa Island! I have prepared a report when you are ready."

"'Massa Island'?" Aly grumbled, unstrapping her seat belt. "Guess they've made themselves comfy."

With a smile, Brother Dimitrios gestured for us to exit. As Aly stepped toward the door, Mustafa stood from his pilot seat, turning toward me. His eyes radiated pure hate. At first I thought his arms were covered with tattoos, but I realized they were bruises from the window I'd shut on him. "This will not be comfy for you," he said in a thick Greek accent.

Brother Dimitrios exhaled. "*Vre*, Brother Mustafa," he said with weary amusement. "Cannot we let bygones be bygones? Serves you right for being trigger-happy."

I felt Mustafa's eyes like lasers burning into my head. As I stepped into the hatch, he shot his arm out and ripped my backpack off my shoulders. "Hey!" I shouted.

Dimitrios clucked wearily. "I will speak to Mustafa about his roughness, Jack. But of course we must have the Loculi. As a precaution, that's all. We will take extraordinary care of them."

As I stepped out onto the tarmac, I felt my heart sinking.

Shake it off, a voice scolded in my brain. *What were you expecting? They'd let you keep them?*

"Jack . . ." Aly said, tugging on my shirt sleeve.

She and Cass were staring at a commotion at the edge of the tarmac, where a line of ragged people in filthy white uniforms was being led out of the jungle. They were heading to one of the supply buildings, whose front door was guarded by two sentries.

"Ah yes, I imagine you know some of these people," Brother Dimitrios said.

I nodded, examining the grim, familiar faces. "Cobb— she worked in the kitchen. Made the salads. The tall guy, Stretch, could repair anything mechanical. Yeah, I know them."

"Good," Dimitrios said. "They will be happy to see you. They are going through the welcoming process."

"In chains?" Aly said.

"Well, they were hostile when we found them," Dimitrios said. "They were among a much larger band of escapees near Mount Onyx."

"What happened to the others?" I asked.

His smile sent a shot of ice up my spine. "Let's just say these are the lucky ones."

CHAPTER TWENTY-THREE

GOOD ENOUGH FOR THE COCKROACHES

I WATCHED THE prisoners being led into the distant building, keeping an eye out for Fiddle's ponytail. I didn't see it. They all looked like their hair had been cut by a lawn mower. I didn't see anyone who resembled him or Nirvana at all.

I was afraid to ask Brother Dimitrios if those two were among the "others."

At the moment, I couldn't ask Dimitrios anything anyway. He was in deep conversation with the woman who'd met him outside the door. She towered over him, looking down a long, bumpy nose, and as she spoke, her silver-black ponytail seemed to wag excitedly. She was yapping away in clipped Greek sentences and gesturing toward us with a bony, olive-green finger.

"Margaret Hamilton," Aly said.

"You know her name?" I said.

"That's the name of the actress who played the Wicked Witch of the West in the *Wizard of Oz* movie," Aly said. "She looks just like her."

The woman looked at us and flashed a snaggletoothed grin. "Cue the flying monkeys," I murmured.

"Jack, this is Almira Gulch," Dimitrios said. "She will be turning you into a newt and eating you for lunch."

No, he didn't actually say that. What he actually said was, "Children, this is Mrs. Petaloude. She is in charge of recruit training. We have a bit of an emergency, alas, so I will be turning you over to one of my associates. Just stay here for a few moments, will you?"

"Wait, *training*?" I said. "Training for what?"

But they were already walking toward a Jeep, with Mrs. Petaloude bending his ear about something.

"Jack, who has the Loculi?" Aly whispered.

"Mustafa," I said.

"One more thing to worry about. I wish your dad hadn't sent them to us." Aly groaned, shaking her head. "I'm thinking about that shard, too. We should rotate it, each of us taking it for a while. To keep ourselves healthy. I'm good for now, and you've been holding it all along. Let's give it to Cass."

Cass turned toward her blankly, as if he hadn't understood

a word. I was worried about him. Since Torquin's death, he had completely checked out.

I pulled the tiny shard from my wallet and slipped it to him. "Can you keep this safe?"

Cass nodded, slipping the shard into his own wallet. I heard the voice of Brother Yiorgos calling us from the edge of the tarmac. He did not look happy, to say the least. His scowl had deepened and his skin had been darkened by the sun. In the deep crags on his face, you could imagine families of mosquitoes frolicking happily. We hadn't exactly left him on good terms. Somewhere in the jungle near Mount Onyx was a tree tattooed with the back of his head, courtesy of Torquin.

"Follow me," he called out. "Now."

"Nice to see you, too," Aly grumbled.

We walked behind him as he tromped down the thick jungle path. He was wearing a bag slung around his shoulder that slapped against his sides as he walked. I swatted away bugs by the dozen. "At least they could give us repellent," I grumbled.

"Brother Yiorgos is repellent," Aly said.

Yiorgos spun around. "I would save up that sense of humor if I were you," he said. "You will need it."

As we moved out of the jungle and into the campus clearing, I could see what Brother Yiorgos meant. Nothing was funny about what the Massa had done here. We'd seen hints of the transformation from the air, but I wasn't prepared for this.

The Karai had fashioned their institute to look like a college—all red-brick buildings with stone steps, connected by grassy lawns and brick pathways. Now the brick paths were being replaced with cement, and the grass patches were being filled with gravel. The Massa attack had totaled a couple of the buildings, and in their place new structures were rising—drab concrete slabs with tiny windows. I was relieved to see that the magnificent, museumlike House of Wenders still stood across the quadrangle. But its sides had been damaged by bombs, and now the bricks were being removed for a makeover. The seven columns still stood at the top of the stairs, but the word *Wenders* had been chiseled from the marble pediment. On the ground, ready to be hoisted into place, was a cement block carved deeply with another word:

"Soon, this will all be perfect," Brother Yiorgos said in his thick Greek accent. "Massa strong. No more like Karai. No more froufrou Harvard-bricky college-la-la-la heads in clouds."

Aly scratched her head. "Could you repeat that?"

Brother Yiorgos grunted, pushing us into a bunkerlike building next to the House of Wenders.

I was sort of hoping we'd go back to our old dorm, which was now surrounded by scaffolding and teeming with Massa workers. Not that the dorm was a cozy place to begin with. But it looked like a palace next to the long metal-sided box they were taking us to now.

The doorknobs contained massive locks and the windows were barred. Inside, the place had the welcoming smell of wet cement and freshly cut tin. Our footsteps clonked on a metal floor as we passed tiny, unfurnished rooms. We had to duck through an open metal doorframe as Yiorgos led us into a large boxy space with a square hole for a window. "Living room," he said.

"Sofas and flat-screen TV arriving tomorrow?" Aly asked.

Yiorgos's eyes blazed. "You are here to work." He zipped open his shoulder bag and threw a pile of clothes onto a metal work table. On top, a white polo shirt unfolded. It had an *M* insignia on the left breast pocket. "Wait for Brother Dimitrios. Wear these. You smell bad."

"Where are we supposed to sit?" Aly asked.

"On the floor," Yiorgos said with a sneer. "If it's good

144

enough for the cockroaches, it's good enough for you."

As he stomped away, Cass turned to the window and stared silently. Around us, the jungle was growing dark. It was hard to believe a whole day had gone by since we'd awakened in Greece.

Aly slumped against the wall. "Okay, Tailor, sew us up something quick. Because I don't like this at all. I have a feeling we out-stupided ourselves by coming here."

"Stay focused," I said resolutely. "The key is finding Fiddle and the rebels. They're still out there. They've got to be."

"You saw those prisoners, Jack," Aly said. "And those are the ones the Massa spared!"

"That's what Brother Dimitrios told us," I said. "And Brother Dimitrios lies. Fiddle rescued a lot of people. Once we find them, we have a team. Experts. Fighters. We take the island back, reconstruct the Loculus of Healing, find the backpack, and book it."

"Five," Aly said, holding up her hand.

As I slapped it, Cass spun around. His face was bright red.

"Are you two serious?" he said, his voice a garbled rasp. "What planet are you on? Do you think we're really going to survive this? *Do you think we deserve to?*"

"Cass . . . ?" Aly said cautiously. She and I exchanged a look. It was the first thing Cass had said since we left Greece.

"They're dead, Jack," Cass said. "They're all dead, like Torquin. Did you see the fires in the jungle? The Massa smoked them out."

"It's just smoke, Cass," Aly said. "It's not proof of anything."

"Think about it, Jack—they escaped with *nothing*, no weapons, no communication, no food!" Cass was practically yelling now. "If the smoke didn't get them, starvation did. Don't you guys see? We're dead people, all of us! This was a terrible plan. They're going to separate us, take what they need from us, and then kill us! They're evil. *Bhegad is dead and Torquin is dead and Fiddle is dead and we're dead!*"

His voice echoed sharply against the metal walls. I felt paralyzed. Tongue-tied. "You—you didn't kill Torquin, Cass," I said lamely. "It wasn't your—"

"If you say that to me one more time, I'll kill you, too!" Cass blurted.

Tears had formed at the corners of his eyes, and he turned back to the window. Aly walked toward him and stood inches away—not touching him, just standing. She took a deep breath. "Hey, you want to know something I never told you?"

"No," Cass said.

"This will sound dumb," she went on, "but my mom was really impressed with you. She's a psychologist, and she really knows how to read people. She said you had an incredibly strong emotional core."

Cass snorted. "You're right. It does sound dumb."

"You know what else she always says?" Aly went on. "Lack of sleep is the number-one thing that can mess up a person's brain. At least fifty percent of all psychological pain can be eased by regular sleep."

Cass turned away.

"We've been up more than twenty-four hours, Cass," Aly said gently.

"I—" Cass's voice broke. "Aly, I can never forgive myself . . ."

"For Torquin. I know. But you can't stay awake the rest of your life because of what happened. Torquin would want you to continue, Cass. He would want you to live. And you need sleep. We all do." Aly knelt on all fours, sweeping aside scraps of metal and bunching up a thick blue plastic sheet. "Come on. We'll catch a nap right here. The Massa Hilton."

I saw a trace of a smile cross Cass's face. He sank to one knee as if gravity had reached up an invisible hand and yanked him down. As I watched him and Aly settle into the makeshift resting spot, my own head began to feel heavy. I slid down against the wall, yawning. "Good night, guys."

"'Night, Jack . . . Aly," Cass squeaked. And then he added, "And I didn't mean what I said, about wanting to kill you."

Aly smiled. "We didn't think so."

* * *

The tap on my shoulder came about ten hours later by the clock, but it felt as if I'd been asleep for fifteen minutes.

As I blinked my eyes open, Brother Dimitrios stared down at me. He looked haggard and tired himself. "So sorry for the interruption . . ."

I yawned. My body was aching. We were all wearing our clean Massa clothing, and the room smelled of laundry detergent and sawdust. "Can we do this later?" I said. "I'm getting used to my new dorm."

With a weary smile, Dimitrios held out his hand. "Oh dear, did Yiorgos tell you this was your dorm? That scalawag. We wouldn't house you in a place like this—it's a temporary way station while your rooms are being prepared. Anyway, I'm afraid that there are some things that you must take care of, Jack."

"Now?" I said. "It's the middle of the night."

Cass was stirring now, and Aly bolted to her feet. "What's going on?" she demanded.

"Go back to sleep," Brother Dimitrios said. "Someone will come soon to take you to your quarters."

"But you just said we had to leave—" Aly began.

"I *said*," Brother Dimitrios snapped, "just Jack."

Aly raced to the doorway and stood there, arms folded. "Sorry, but no."

"Excuse me?" Brother Dimitrios said with a curious smile.

"We go together," Aly replied. "You've already brainwashed Marco, and you can't have Jack. So, no."

Cass looked at her in amazement. "You go, girl."

"I assure you, dear Aly, brainwashing is the furthest thing from my mind," Brother Dimitrios said. "You three are very different people with different talents. We must interview each of you, to develop individual plans. Surely you can't expect to stand over each other's shoulders forever."

"You need us, Dimitrios," Aly said. "So here are our terms. Jack stays. You bring Marco to us, show us he's still alive. We talk to Marco for an hour. Privately. *Then* we negotiate."

Brother Dimitrios looked confused. "Yes, we do need you. But I daresay you need us more. And for us to help you—to preserve your lives, my dear—we must follow our orders or *we* suffer consequences—"

"What consequences?" Aly demanded. "And who gives them?"

"So if you'll pardon my rudeness, here are *my* terms," Dimitrios barreled on. "If Jack expects to see you—and his father—again, he will do as I say and come with me. Alone."

CHAPTER TWENTY-FOUR
THE ILLUSION OF CONTROL

AS WE PASSED the place of eating we used to call the Comestibule, two horrifying things happened:

One, the sun peeked over the horizon. Which meant we were officially going to begin a full day of misery in Massaville.

Two, the smell of coffee and fried eggs from inside the building actually made me drool. As in, a string of liquid escaped my mouth and made a straight line down to my shoes. "You are ailing?" Brother Dimitrios said.

"I am hungry," I replied, wiping my mouth.

"The cafeteria is not yet open," he said, "but I have some pull here. You will need nourishment for what we have planned."

"Okay, enough mystery," I said. "What's the plan?"

But Brother Dimitrios was already heading into the building.

Seeing the interior was a shock. The place looked totally different. The paintings and the huge antler chandelier were gone, and all the wood paneling had been painted white. Brother Mustafa the pilot was swigging down some coffee, but he left the moment we arrived. Dimitrios snapped his fingers and immediately a sleepy-looking goon with a runny nose padded into the room, setting a plate of food in front of me.

I stared down at a yellow lump oozing about a pound of smelly white cheese.

"Chef's specialty, feta omelet," Brother Dimitrios explained.

"I think I just lost my appetite," I said. "Do you have any cereal?"

Brother Dimitrios leaped up from his seat, running into the kitchen to demand another meal. As I pushed the plate aside, I looked around the room.

Memories flooded in. I pictured the great banner that had once been strung across this hall: WELCOME TO YOUR KARAI INSTITUTE HOME, JACK. Back then I'd been too scared and creeped out to appreciate the welcome. Or the food.

Dimitrios reappeared with a bowl of soggy granola and

some weird-tasting milk. I bolted them down. I was still chewing as we walked out the back door. We hadn't gone ten feet before I saw something that made me nearly spit out the remains of my breakfast.

The KI game building, where we used to have unlimited entertainment possibilities, had been gutted. Now it was being merged with the enormous hangar building next to it—the place where all the KI repairs used to take place. It was where I had nearly been hit on the head by Fritz the mechanic because of my own clumsiness.

Its roof had been raised even higher. It was a fretwork of curved, thick wooden beams, and I could see that the building's final shape would be like a gigantic egg. All around the building, massive cranes made of lashed-together tree trunks groaned loudly, hoisting beams on steel winches.

"Behold the future Tharrodrome," Brother Dimitrios said. "From the word *tharros*, which means 'courage.' Perhaps you will remember our task chamber in the compound in Egypt, where your remarkable friend Marco performed some extraordinary feats of strength."

I did remember the chamber. And I remembered what the Massa had unleashed on Marco. A mutant beast. A warrior swordsman. "Is that what you're building here? A place where you torture kids and put their lives at risk?"

"A place where we test our Select and grow them to their

full potential," Brother Dimitrios said. "Which the KI, in their foolishness, never thought to do."

"Why did you bring me here alone?" I asked.

Brother Dimitrios opened a wood-frame, windowless door. "For your test, of course."

I stepped inside. The room had a coffee machine, a sink, a door, two office chairs, a wall clock, and a desk. I figured the door led to a toilet. A string of curly fluorescent lights hung from the unfinished ceiling. On the desk was a tablet with a keyboard. A slideshow flashed on the screen—photo after photo of Massa goons tearing down the Karai Institute. "So this is it?" I said. "I have to watch the construction of Six Flags Over Horrorland?"

"Sit, please." Brother Dimitrios rolled back the office chair. As I sat, he opened a desk drawer and pulled out a set of earplugs connected to a small tablet. "During your task, you will wear these, with the tablet hooked onto your belt. This way you can communicate with me if you need to."

"Wait. Where will you be?" I asked.

"This does not matter," Dimitrios said. "Let us begin."

He touched the screen. The slideshow disappeared to reveal a screen full of strange-looking apps with Greek labels. "Do I get a lifeline?" I asked. "If it involves any tech, I'll need Aly."

"You, Jack, will be *their* lifeline." Dimitrios leaned over and tapped an app that resembled a camera. Instantly the screen showed Aly and Cass in a dorm room, much nicer than the one we'd just been inside. Cass was holding a phone and Aly was touching her fingers to the wall.

"Aly appears to be placing a wad of chewing gum over a spy lens," Brother Dimitrios said. "We placed three of those lenses in the room—small, dark globes about a quarter inch in diameter. Just large enough for a bright young person to spot. You see, she believes she is blocking us from seeing into the room."

"Because the lenses are fake," I said.

"Very good, Jack," Dimitrios said. "This is our way of giving her the illusion of control."

"If the lenses don't work, how come we see Cass and Aly?" I asked.

"We are actually watching through another lens, the size of a pinhead," Dimitrios replied. "It blends in with the grains of cement on the ceiling. I would like you to keep an eye on your friends. If they try anything funny, they will ruin your test. And there will be consequences. Oh, yes, just in case . . ."

He tapped another app and a kidney-shaped map appeared on the screen. In the northern section, two dots glowed. "This, of course, is the island, and the dots are Cass and Aly. Should they move outside the cabin, you will be able to track their movements."

"That's my trial—to spy on my own friends?" I asked.

Brother Dimitrios shook his head. "Your trial is to decode this."

Another app, this one revealing an image of an old document.

In hexad de heptimus veritas.

X is the spot where
Our youth became
Old.

Where foolishness
Quickened the
Evil foretold.
Immortal Atlantis
May kill once again.
For deep within orbits
Will curses remain.

"What the heck does that mean?" I asked.

"You tell me," Brother Dimitrios said.

"Wait," I said. "I have to do *your* work? You guys couldn't figure this out?"

"Who says we haven't?" Brother Dimitrios shot back.

"Any hints?" I said.

"The answer to this is the name of a great danger that exists on this island." Dimitrios held a remote to the wall clock. It instantly became a timer, which read 20:00:00.

"You have twenty minutes," he said. "If you fail, one of your friends dies."

"Wait, you're joking, right?" I said. "You wouldn't do that. You said you needed us!"

"Unfortunately, Jack, I am not the one who sets the rules," Dimitrios said.

"Then who is it?" I demanded. *"Let me talk to him now!"*

Dimitrios backed out of the room shaking his head. "I am sorry, dear boy. But twenty-three seconds have gone by."

The door clicked shut as he disappeared.

CHAPTER TWENTY-FIVE
In Hexad de Heptimus Veritas

17:58:13.

This was insane.

Impossible.

I couldn't concentrate. My eyebrows were raining sweat. Nearly two whole minutes had gone by and I hadn't done a thing except stare at the dumb poem. I couldn't make any sense of it.

Curses? Deep within orbits?

Youth became old?

The words swirled in my head until they had no meaning at all. Like I was looking at a foreign language.

Do something. Print it out. Take notes. First things that come to mind.

That was what my creative writing teacher, Mr. Linker, always told us. *Sometimes it looks different when it's on paper.* So I went to work.

In hexad de heptimus veritas.

X is the spot where
Our youth became
Old.
Where foolishness
Quickened the
Evil foretold.
Immortal Atlantis
May kill once again.
For deep within orbits
Will curses remain.

I felt like an utter idiot.

This was a waste of time.

15:56:48.

"Code . . . it's a code, it must be a code . . ." Now I was talking to myself.

I thought about the codes we'd seen.

The rock at the top of Mount Onyx.

No. Not like this at all.

The door to the Hanging Gardens of Babylon.

Nope.

The letter from Charles Newton we'd found at the Mausoleum at Halicarnassus.

Uh-uh.

Wait.

I stared at the heading, which was in bigger type than the rest of it. *In hexad de heptimus veritas.*

The Charles Newton letter had a heading, too. It was the key to understanding the rest of the letter. Where the date was supposed to be, there was a message: *The 7th, to the end.* That meant we had to count every seventh letter.

My eyes fixed on the word *Heptimus.* It was like Heptakiklos.

Hepta was seven; *kiklos* was circle.

I wiped the sweat from my brow. *Duh.* So much of this quest was about the number seven. Everything always came back to sevens.

Carefully I wrote down every seventh letter of the poem.

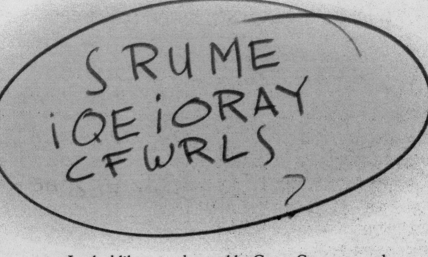

Looked like a word scramble. Great. Cass was good at those. Probably Aly, too. For all I knew, Marco ate them for lunch. Me? It's about the same level as my gift for ballet dancing. Zero out of ten in the Jack McKinley Scale of Loserdom.

But Brother Dimitrios's words clattered around in my brain: *If you fail, one of your friends dies.*

The threat of murder has a way of bringing out the best in a person.

Okay, the *Q* had to go with a *U*. In the letters I saw a *query* . . . also a *require* . . . and an *I am* . . . I began scribbling as fast as I could:

160

WARM SQUIRRELS, ICY FOE

MY CALF WORRIES SQUIRE

FORMERLY ICIER SQUAWS

i SCARE SQUIRMY FLOWER

SORCERER QUALIFY SWIM

ACQUIRE LESS FROM WIRY

MR. WOLF iS QUEASY CRIER

"Arrrghhh!" I cried out.
Useless. I slammed down my pen.

161

7:58:34.

Eight whole minutes, down the toilet!

Okay. Calm down.

I needed to go further. Figure out the other parts of that heading. *In hexad de heptimus veritas.* My fingers shook as I opened the tablet's browser. I typed "in hexad de heptimus veritas" into a search engine page but got nothing. So I entered the words one by one.

Definition: hexad. A group of six.

Definition: heptimus. Sevenths.

Definition: veritas. Truth.

This was weird. The first two words were from the Greek, the last was from Latin. It was a mishmash. This wasn't Atlantean. Or even ancient. Brother Dimitrios and his pals must have made it up.

"Just go with it, Jack," I muttered to myself. "Okay . . . in a group of six of sevenths truth . . ."

7:14:32 . . .

I glanced away from the clock and then back again.

7:14:29 . . .

7:14:28 . . .

Seven-one-four-two-eight.

For that one second, the clock showed a number that meant something to me—the magic sequence of sevenths, 714285!

I hated fraction conversions. But I knew this one cold.

Divide seven into any single digit. You get the same

digits in the same sequence. Well, they may start in a different place, but it's all the same.

Like .142857. Which is one seventh.

Or .285714, two sevenths.

Or .428571, three sevenths.

Or .714285—five sevenths, same as on the clock.

The same six digits over and over again, starting in different places.

That would be a group of six.

A hexad!

We were getting somewhere. Maybe.

In hexad de heptimus veritas.

Okay.

That would mean . . . *Truth in the hexad of the sevenths.*

But which hexad?

I figured, start with one seventh: .142857. Maybe if I pulled out the right letters, it would spell something. So the first letter, the fourth, the second, the eighth, and so on from each line. . . .

Impossible. One of the lines only had three letters.

Wait. Wait.

There was another possibility.

Down the side of the printout, I wrote out the magic sequence, one digit for each line of text. Then I circled the corresponding letter—for number 1, the first letter, for number 4, the fourth . . .

In hexad de heptimus veritas.

1   X is the spot where

4   Our youth became

2   Old.

8   Where foolishness

5   Quickened the

7   Evil foretold.

1   Immortal Atlantis

4   May kill once again.

2   For deep within orbits

8   Will curses remain.

Underneath I wrote out the letters:

XYLOKRIKOS

"What the heck?" I quickly typed the word into the search engine. The first hit made me gasp:

164

Der Xylokrikos

Xylokrikos—jungle creature—Journals, Herman Wenders
Von "Xylos" (Holz) und "Krikos" (Kreis), ein sagenhaftes Geschöpf
der Mythologie selten angeführt. Entstehen der Kreise von Jahresringen

I clicked on it and looked at the page:

DER XYLOKRIKOS

Von "Xylos" (Holz) und "Krikos" (Kreis), ein sagenhaftes
Geschöpf, in Erzählungen der Mythologie selten angeführt.
Entstehen der Kreise von Jahresringen im Baumstumpf.

Finally I clicked on the translation button and read what it meant:

THE XYLOKRIKOS

From xylos (wood) and krikos (ring), a mythological figure rarely sighted by sources. Arises from the rings of a tree stump.

I leaped up from my seat, pumping my fist in the air. *"Woo-hoo! I got it! Brother Dimitrios, I know you must be watching this! The answer is Xylokrikos!"*

Dimitrios's face appeared on the tablet screen. I jumped. I didn't realize he was controlling the screen like that. "Ah, bravo, Jack," he said.

"Thanks," I said quickly. "So you'll let them alone, right? Cass and Aly—they're going to be okay?"

"For now," Dimitrios said. "Your friends will indeed be pleased that you passed part one. Let's tell them."

The image dissolved. Now I was looking into Cass and Aly's room.

It was empty.

"Well, will you look at that . . . tsk-tsk-tsk," came Dimitrios's voice.

"Where did they go?" I demanded. *"If you hurt them . . ."*

166

"They are fine. I am a man of my word," Dimitrios said. "Ten minutes ago they received a handwritten message from a fellow named Fiddle."

I froze up but said nothing.

"It seems this musically named fellow directed them toward somewhere on the island," Dimitrios continued.

The screen's image dissolved to reveal a patch of jungle. "You have hidden cameras?"

"All throughout the island, of course," Dimitrios said.

In the midst of the patch was a dull glow. As the camera zoomed in, the glow became a hatch, half-hidden by vines. On it was a carved Λ.

"Don't get too excited," Dimitrios said. "If they reach this hatch, there is a . . . surprise waiting for them."

"What *kind* of surprise?" I demanded.

"You will be given sufficient information to figure that out."

"Just tell me if they're in danger!" I said.

"I would recommend that you make haste, Jack," Dimitrios replied.

The image vanished. In place of Brother Dimitrios's face was a map of the island, marked like a radar screen. I could see two blue dots moving from one of the compound buildings into the jungle, toward a big *X*.

Farther south in the compound was a third blue dot. As I walked the tablet to the door, the dot jiggled slightly.

It was me.

"You will be allowed one lifeline," Brother Dimitrios's voice said. "And that will be me. You may ask one question after you begin."

"What am I supposed to do?" I shouted into the tablet. *"And that doesn't count as my lifeline question!"*

Dimitrios's answer was one word:

"Hurry."

CHAPTER TWENTY-SIX
LIFELINE

"UCCCHH." I STOOPED down and plucked the tablet out of the jungle grass.

I was running too fast, being too hasty. The jungle humidity drenched me. My hands were slippery. I needed the tablet to check my bearings, my blue dots, but I kept dropping it.

Where were they?

There.

Their two dots were looping around from the north. They'd had a big head start, and they were way closer to the hatch than I was. My dot was at the extreme western part of the screen. I'd never catch up to them. I'd have to go straight to the hatch.

Clutching tight to the tablet, I ran. I lifted my feet as high as they could go. Overhead, birds and monkeys screeched as if they were watching a soccer match. As I got closer I shouted, *"Aly! Cass!"*

My answer was a chorus of hoots, caws, and shrieks. My friends were never going to hear me.

My blue dot moved toward the goal faster than Aly's and Cass's did from the north. When I was on top of the big *X*, I stopped.

I looked around for a hatch, but all I saw was the same old jungle mess. I leaned over, clearing away brush with my arms. A snake hissed, slithering away. A huge lizard eyed me from beneath a nearby bush.

"Where is it?" I cried out in frustration.

EEEEEE! came the shriek of a monkey. Torquin had understood those cries. He'd made friends with some of these creatures. What were they telling me?

My eyes were watery and stinging. I didn't know if it was sweat or tears. I caught sight of the corner of a high tree stump and leaned on it, rubbing away the moisture with my free hand.

EEEE-EEE-EEEEEE!

EEEEEEE!

I had to jump back. Monkeys were dropping out of the trees like parachute jumpers. They landed just beyond the stump in two lines.

I narrowed my eyes. "What do you guys want?"

EEEE-EEE-EEEEEE! One of the chimps pointed to the stump, slapping his head.

"It's a stump! What's wrong with . . . ?" *The research.* I realized Brother Dimitrios had given me a big fat clue. "Okay . . . the xylokrikos . . . is that what you're warning me about? This thing is really a monster?"

I stared at the remnant of the old tree. Was this where Brother Dimitrios was leading us all—some kind of portal, where the monster would morph out of the wood to attack us?

I backed away. But then, out of nowhere, a rock went flying past my ear. The monkeys were trying to get my attention. They were divided down the middle into two groups, each screaming and gesturing toward the other.

"What?" I said. "Come on. This is a magical island. Be magical. *Talk to me!*"

They were pointing to something between them. I stepped closer until I could see a silvery filament like a taut spiderweb, a line so thin that it was barely a shimmer. It emerged from the jungle behind them and seemed to be connected somewhere near me, like some weird zip line for insects. Squinting against the sunlight that flashed through the trees, I followed the line to its source.

It ended at the stump.

From their reactions, I thought the monkeys were going

to have a heart attack. At the place where the filament attached to the trunk's bark was a set of metal electrodes.

An electric fence. That's what it had to be. Back when we were first on the island, Aly had discovered a network of these, placed by the KI around the campus.

How extensive was this fence? How far away were Cass and Aly? I checked my tablet, lining up my location with theirs.

I was at the bottom right of the *X*. Aly and Cass were coming closer to the top left. They would be crossing the *X* soon. But the monkeys were all here, all warning *me*.

"Lifeline!" I screamed into the tablet. "What is this— this *wire*, Dimitrios? Where does it go, and what does it do?"

Dimitrios's face did not appear. Instead, I saw footage of Aly and Cass tromping through the woods. This was his answer: a video feed from some hidden security camera in a tree. They were headed for a broken-down cottage in the distance. Around the cottage was a perfectly round wooden fence.

You will be given sufficient information to figure that out.

That's what Dimitrios had promised me. But this information was wack. How was any of this meaningful? Screaming monkeys, electric filaments, hatches that didn't exist, tree-stump monsters . . .

The xylokrikos.

From xylos *("wood") and* krikos *("ring") . . .*

No. It wasn't about the stump monster. Not really. It was about its name—wood plus ring. A ring of wood!

The fence.

That was what the poem's code meant.

"It's not about a monster, is it, Dimitrios?" I shouted. "The puzzle—xylokrikos was the answer. But it's about that wooden fence. The wire is attached—and if they cross it they'll be electrocuted! *How do I turn it off? Lifeline! Lifeline! How do I turn it off!"*

A soft chuckle arose from my tablet. "I said one question, and you just asked three. Well, I have a heart and I shall address the last one. The only way to de-electrify that filament is to break the circuit. It is constructed of carbene, an extremely thin, extremely strong material developed by our scientists. So you will not be able to break it with, say, a stick. I suppose the only way to disable it would be contact with a grounded water-containing carbon unit that will conduct the electricity."

"Meaning what?" I demanded.

"A living being, Jack," Dimitrios replied. "There are candidates in your vicinity, I'd say."

The monkeys were backing away, hopping and gesticulating, slapping themselves obliviously. If I could trap one of them . . .

No. They seemed to sense what I was thinking and were

already in retreat. I'd never be able to do it in time.

But letting Cass or Aly touch that fence was worse.

Unless I did it first.

I closed my eyes. This was the right thing to do. I was the Tailor, who figured things out. I was the Destroyer. In this one act, I would be both.

People say your life flashes before your eyes just before you die. Not me. All I could see was the photo on my old hand mirror—Dad, Mom, and me as a toddler in the snow, playing Boom to Daddy. The photo I'd been looking at every day of my life since Mom disappeared. It calmed me down. Made me realize I'd once had some happiness in my life.

I would be dead in a few seconds. But at least I was smiling.

Stretching out my arms, I dropped the tablet.

And I dived into the filament, chest first.

CHAPTER TWENTY-SEVEN

THE SEVENTH CODEX

MY FIRST TASTE of death was a mouthful of wet leaves.

I sprang up. My feet were still on the jungle ground. The monkeys were still chattering. My eyes darted toward the tree stump. I saw the black electrodes where the filament had been attached.

Just the electrodes. Nothing else. The unbreakable carbene filament was . . . *broken*? "No . . ." I murmured.

They'd touched it first. They'd gotten to it before I had. I'd been too slow to save my friends' lives.

"Aly! Cass!" I screamed.

The monkeys screeched back at me. But they were hiding now, no longer helping me. Without seeing them, I didn't know where the filament had been. I had no idea where to go. Everything in the jungle looked the same.

I scrambled for the tablet, scooping it off the ground. The screen was cracked, and pressing the power button did absolutely nothing. Tossing it into the jungle, I reared back my head and shouted Brother Dimitrios's name.

Among the cacophony of monkeys and birds, I heard a woman's voice directly behind me. "Remarkable. I would not have predicted it would have been this one."

I spun around but all I could see was a suffocating scrim of dense greenery all around. *"Who are you?"* I shouted. *"Where are Aly and Cass?"*

"Remarkable indeed. He is still concerned about them. Bravo." Dimitrios emerged, with an enormous smile. Next to him was a woman in commando gear. From the weathered wrinkles on her face, I could tell she was much older than Mom. But her carriage was straight and upright like a soldier's, her eyes sharp and smart. Despite her advanced years she looked as if she could handle herself against anyone.

"First," the lady said, "be assured that your friends are safe."

"Wh-what?" I stammered. "If they . . . then I should be . . ."

"The filament held no electrical charge," Brother Dimitrios said.

I wasn't sure I heard that right. "Wait. It was a fake? *You made me think I was going to die?"*

"It seems inscrutable, I know," the woman replied, "but it was necessary."

"And who are *you*?" I demanded.

Dimitrios stepped forward. "Jack, my boy, I know this is upsetting but manners are always important when among your elders. Before you is—"

The woman held up her hand to quiet Dimitrios. "You may call me Number One," she said.

"Wait . . . Number One?" I said. Okay, maybe it was just the shock of being alive. Or the distant ridiculous jabbering of monkeys. Or the solemn way she called herself a potty name. But I started laughing like a five-year-old. "That's your name—Number One? I mean, really, *Number One?*"

"It's more of a rank, I suppose," she said with a bemused smile.

"I guess it could be worse—*you could be called Number Two!*" I was howling now. "That would really be rank!"

"Jack, stop that now!" Dimitrios said. "Apologize!"

"Sorry . . . sorry," I replied, taking deep breaths.

I expected Number One to be as stuffy and upset as Dimitrios. But she was smiling curiously at me. "I had a brother once," she said. "You remind me of him."

"So. Number One," I said. "Nice to meet you. How come I haven't ever seen you before?"

"I haven't needed to be seen until now." She nodded

toward Dimitrios, then turned back toward the campus. "We have much to talk about. Follow me, please."

I stood my ground, looking at the back of her head in disbelief. My giddy mood was curdling fast. Into rage. "Okay. Just a second. You nearly scared me to death. You owe me an explanation. I want to see my friends. I want to talk now."

I heard a rustling in the bushes behind me. Brother Yiorgos emerged, blocking my path, along with another goon who wore an eyepatch. Neither was smiling.

"You know Yiorgos, of course," Brother Dimitrios said. "And this is Brother Plutarchos—er, Cyclops, for short."

"Enough. Your friends are fine. Come. I am not fond of mosquitoes, Jack." The woman turned to go, calling over her shoulder, "And you, I suspect, are not fond of being carried."

* * *

I had a bad case of WWF, Walking While Furious. I could barely see straight. My heart was like a jackhammer.

I wanted to find Cass and Aly, tell them the story, and begin an assault on the Massa—*somehow.* But whenever I slowed down, Yiorgos began breathing down my neck. Which, trust me, is enough to keep anyone moving.

The woman led us through the jungle, into the campus, and up the stairs of the building formerly known as the House of Wenders. I barely recognized the lobby. During the KI days, it had been a soaring, dark-wood-paneled atrium with a towering dinosaur skeleton. Now it was a construction site. The skeleton had been removed, and the grand mahogany balcony was shattered and patched up with crudely cut wooden planks.

"We sustained quite a bit of damage," she said.

"In the attack *you* caused," I reminded her.

She smiled. "Ah well, the old fortress needed some sprucing up anyway."

As I followed her to the second floor, I felt a tug in my chest. She'd taken over Professor Bhegad's office, complete with his rickety old leather chair and wooden desk. His mess was gone—no more piles of papers and bursting file cabinets. No more creaky, dust-encrusted metal fan and grimy windows. But the old Oriental rug remained, and I could see a straight path worn by Bhegad's footsteps, leading from desk to door.

Somehow the sight of that path brought him back in my mind. I could see his heavy footfalls and stooped gait, the way he pushed his glasses up his bulbous nose, his stiff and formal language. Here in this office, on the day Marco had fallen into the volcano to save our lives, the professor had actually cried. For us.

For the first time, I realized how much I missed the old guy.

"Sit," the woman said, gesturing toward an empty chair.

Looking straight at this gray-eyed Massa leader, I wondered if she could cry. I wondered if she had emotions about anything.

Just over her shoulder were two framed black-and-white photos. One, of a dark-eyed boy, looked like a faded school picture. The other was a dark-curly-haired man with watery eyes and a huge, ridiculous-looking smile.

"Family resemblance, no?" the woman said. "Both my father and my brother are long gone."

"Did you play chicken with their lives, too?" I muttered.

The woman raised an eyebrow. "Excuse me?"

I didn't care if she was an adult, or if that ridiculous name "Number One" meant she was the head of the Massa or Queen of the Universe. For all I knew, those family photos were just more lies. *I thought I was going to die!* I rose to my feet and gripped the edge of her desk. "The poem was a lie. The code was a lie. The xylokrikos meant nothing, and you made up that stuff about the unbreakable wire. Was that your idea of a joke?"

Brother Yiorgos grabbed me and held my arms behind my back. The lady known as Number One stood up sharply. "Release him. He's more angry than dangerous."

With a grunt, the monk pushed me down into a chair. Number One came around her desk, sat on the edge, and leaned toward me. When she spoke, her voice was soft and sad. "Until you have experienced the death of your own blood before your eyes, you will not appreciate what it means to love and lose someone."

"What makes you think I don't know that?" I snapped.

I looked away so I wouldn't be tempted to blurt out any truths about my mother.

"If you do know, then we may begin to understand each other." The woman stood, looking at the two pictures on the wall. "My brother's name was Osman. He and you were very much alike. He was a Select, you know. There is not a day that I don't think of him."

"Your brother was a Select?" I said. "So you knew about all of this back then?"

"I did," Number One said. "In fact, I lost both Osman and Father to Artemisia, just as you lost Radamanthus Bhegad."

I thought of Bhegad's soul being ripped from his body. I thought of the last time I'd seen him, hanging from my ankle as I flew on a griffin. I began to shake. In my mind's eye he was falling to the earth below, falling fast, without a scream . . .

"We have the resources to prevent further deaths, Jack," the woman said, her voice softening. "To restore the world to its glorious destiny that ended at the fall of Atlantis—reason and equality, health and progress, cooperation. Since the fall, the world has become a battleground among barbarians, all of them blind to the coming destruction. You are our hope, Jack. Show him, Dimitrios."

Brother Dimitrios spun a tablet toward me.

"Does this look familiar?" the woman asked.

"Yes," I said. "There were a bunch of these paintings at Brother Dimitrios's monastery in Rhodes—all about the life of Massarym."

"Now look at this," Number One added, swiping the screen with a bony finger and revealing another image:

"The two images are the same painting," Dimitrios explained. "In this image, I used infrared imaging to reveal the pentimento."

"Penti-*who*?" I said.

"When words are written onto a canvas, and then artists paint over these words to hide them," Brother Dimitrios said. "That is *pentimento*. The history of Atlantis was written in six books, or codices. Massarym, fearing these books would be destroyed, wrote his own history. We call it the Seventh Codex. And it is hidden in these paintings."

"The Seventh Codex," Number One went on, "told of two curses. When Massarym stole and hid the Loculi for their safekeeping, Uhla'ar blamed his son for the kingdom's destruction. He suspected Massarym wanted to rebuild a new Atlantis with himself as king. Massarym tried to explain the truth: that the queen's tampering had upset the balance of Atlantean power—that he, Massarym, merely wanted to preserve the Loculi. But Uhla'ar would not hear of it. He placed a curse on his own son, that Massarym would never live to see the Loculi retrieved."

"Well, that sure happened," I said.

"Ah, but Massarym, in turn, placed a curse on his father," Number One said. "Uhla'ar would not die, but would be condemned to remain on earth, neither dead nor alive."

"He turned Uhla'ar into a ghost?" I asked.

Brother Dimitrios chanted as if reciting by memory. "'The Curse of Uhla'ar shall not be lifted until the seven Loculi are placed within the Heptakiklos by the actions of the Rightful Ruler. Only then shall the Curse be lifted and the continent raised once again.'"

"Wait—*raised*?" I said. "Like, this whole island? Right here?"

Number One was beaming. "Kind of quickens the heart, doesn't it?"

"Okay . . . okay . . ." I said, trying to make sense of what she'd just said. "Uhla'ar chased Massarym—right, I know that because I have these weird dreams about the past. But about the Loculi. I thought we just had to bring them back and put them in the Heptakiklos. Bam, done and done. No one told us about any Rightful Ruler."

"Dimitrios, continue," Number One commanded.

"'By two indicators shall the Ruler's identity be revealed,'" Brother Dimitrios recited. "'The first shall be an act of Locular destruction. The second, an act of self-sacrifice.'"

I flopped back into my chair. "Oh, great—he's the only one who can activate the Loculi. But he has to destroy one, and then kill himself. Sure. I think I know where you're going with this."

"It is a paradox," Brother Dimitrios said.

"Massarym was all about mysteries," Number One said. "One must read the prophecy carefully, in the original language. *Destruction* sounds so final in English. But broken things can be fixed, no? And what if the act of self-sacrifice is just that—an *act*? An *attempt*."

I closed my eyes and took a deep breath, trying to piece this craziness together. "So you saw me throw the Loculus under the train. Boom, Locular destruction. And just now, you faked me out to see if *I* would *attempt* to sacrifice myself."

They both nodded.

"Didn't you try this with Marco already?" I snapped. "Back in Babylon, he told us *he* was going to be king. Is this your trick—you tell him, then me, then Cass, then Aly . . . ?"

Brother Dimitrios sighed. "You will forgive us for being impulsive about Marco. We had heard how jumped into a volcano for his friends. In our judgment, he had fulfilled the second part of the prophecy—"

"He didn't jump," I said. "He was fighting a vromaski, and they both fell off the edge."

"So we learned," Brother Dimitrios said. "But alas, only later on. So when in Ancient Babylon, he *destroyed a Loculus*, well, that was the first part of the prophecy! But there, too, we were wrong. He merely destroyed the replacement, your so-called Shelley."

"He never destroyed a Loculus," Number One said. "You did, Jack."

I thought about what happened when I was standing by the tracks in New York City, invisible—when Mom was looking straight at me, somehow knowing I was there.

The first to leave the scene had been Dimitrios, muttering something under his breath. We all heard what he'd said—Cass, Aly, and me. Mom had waited till he was gone—and then she'd pointed at me.

I recited those words under my breath. "The Destroyer . . ." I said, repeating Brother Dimitrios's words, "shall rule."

"You have fulfilled both requirements, Jack the Destroyer," the woman said. "Marco has indeed an extraordinary destiny based on his gifts, and Aly and Cass on theirs. But yours is the most important gift of all."

Brother Dimitrios's eyes were intense. "We must keep this a secret until the training is complete."

"And then the real work can begin"—Number One's mouth curved upward into a smile that was half ironic, half admiring—"my liege."

CHAPTER TWENTY-EIGHT

HIS JACKNESS

THERE'S A FINE line between destiny and doofusness, and I was walking it.

All the way back to the dorm, I felt like two people. One of them was trembling with excitement and the other was cackling out loud.

My liege.

Was that supposed to be a joke? Was she flattering me? What did her little smile mean?

And really, what did that painting say? For all I knew, the words in that painting could have been anything—a diary, an Atlantean laundry list, whatever. Did it make any sense that out of the zillion people born in the world since the sinking of Atlantis, I, Jack McKinley the Painfully

Average, would be the future king?

No, it didn't make sense. But neither did magic beach balls, or invisibility, or living statues, or time rifts, or zombies, or acid-spitting creatures.

My worn-out sandal clipped a vine, and I nearly fell over. Massa construction workers looked up and stared at me weirdly. Did they know? Maybe the good news had been sent out to them over some kind of Massaweb. What were they thinking?

All hail, King Jack!

His Royal Highness, Jack the First of Belleville!

A good day to His Jackness, Master of the Kingdom of Atlantis and Ruler of the World!

Sooner or later everyone was going to have to adjust to King Jack. Including me.

I stood up, drew myself up to full height, and gave them a kingly wave with a cupped palm. "Carry on!"

And then one of my new subjects spoke:

"Uh, kid, you just stepped in monkey turds."

* * *

Cass was the first to run toward me from the dorm. "Did they suck out your brains and replace them with Jell-O?"

"Did you see Marco?" Aly asked, her face full of excitement and hope.

"No and no," I said.

Cass crinkled up his face. "What stinks?"

The last hint of kingliness flew out of my head. I wiped my sandals in a wet, grassy spot. "Sorry, I thought I got it all off."

"We need to talk, now," Aly said. "And here, where no one will hear us."

"And fast, because we're starving and the cafeteria's open," Cass said.

"I guess you're feeling better," I said.

Cass nodded. "Oh. That. Yeah, well, sorry about yesterday. Aly and I have been talking. She was right. I'm not going to blame myself, and I'll promise to be more like Torquin. The bravery part, not the grunting and bad driving."

Aly looked like she would explode from excitement. "Jack, we want to hear about your meeting with Brother Creepo. But we have to tell you what happened to us. We got this note from—"

"Not here." I looked around, thinking about the secret cameras the Massa had planted in the jungle. "There are bugs."

"In the trees?" Cass asked.

"My room is safe," Aly said, turning to go back into the dorm. "Leave the sandals and follow me. I destroyed the surveillance cameras."

"Not all of them," I said. "There's one the size of a

pinhead, probably up where the wall meets the ceiling, directly above your desk."

Aly turned back. "Excuse me? How do you—?"

"I'll help you disable it," I said. "Show me the way."

I kicked off my stinky sandals and followed Cass and Aly into the new dorm. It was about twice the size of the old building. Instead of being greeted in a cramped hallway by our old Karai guard, Conan the Armed and Sleepy, there was a big empty entryway two floors high. A hallway led to the right, and I found a door marked with my name. I ducked inside to look. It was a big corner room with screened windows, tons of sunlight, and a shelf with a few used books and an iPod dock. I think the dresser had been Marco's in the old dorm, because one of the drawers had been kicked in and repaired with glue.

I could hear Cass and Aly clomping into the room next to me. I washed my feet, then put on a new pair of sandals I found in the closet and sprinted to meet them. Aly was standing on her desk, staring at me as I entered. In her hand was a piece of twisted metal. Just above her, wires jutted from a spot near the roof. "How did you know, Jack? About this camera?"

"Dimitrios showed me," I said. "The other lenses that you covered with gum? Those were fakes. I was tracking you. They made me think you were in danger."

"Jack, you're scaring me," Cass said.

Aly stepped down, eyeing me warily. "So, that note from Fiddle—?"

"A fake, too," I said. "The Massa led you to that hatch. They made me watch. They told me you were going to be killed. But they were lying. They were testing me. To see if I would sacrifice myself to save your lives."

They both stared at me silently.

"Well . . . ?" Cass asked softly. "Did you?"

I nodded.

"So . . . they're brainwashing you," Aly said.

Cass shrugged. "Sounds like bravery to me."

"It's called behavior modification," Aly barreled on. "You see it in a million movies. They make you feel like you're going to die. Or that someone you love is going to die. They start breaking down your free will. After a while you don't know what's real or fake. Then they can worm their way into your brain and make you believe anything. Like the *Manchurian Candidate*."

"The *who*?" I said.

Aly rolled her eyes. "Classic movie. Don't you have any culture?"

"Don't you ever watch any *new* movies?" Cass replied.

"The point is, the Massa are sneaky and weird." Aly went on. "They deluded Marco into thinking he's going to be the next king. Watch it, Jack. They're probably working on you, too. I think they're trying to separate us—divide and conquer."

"What exactly did they say to you?" Cass asked.

Number One's words burned in my brain: *We must keep this a secret until the training is complete.*

No way. I needed to tell Cass and Aly the truth. Once you start lying to your best friends, it's hard to go back. But right this moment, I didn't know what was true and what wasn't. What if I really did tell them that Number One anointed me future king? They'd say I was a sucker and a traitor, like Marco.

And I wasn't.

I had to think this through myself. Calmly. Without being influenced.

If what Number One told me was a lie, then nothing changed. But if it was true, I had to do it right. I needed to be very, very cautious.

"Well," I said, "it turns out that the head of the Massa is this woman called Number One. She's, like, my grandmother's age—"

"Wait," Aly said. "You met the *head* of the Massa? Just you? Why?"

"I'm special, I guess." I wanted that to sound like a joke, but I'm not sure it worked. "I think she wants to raise the continent of Atlantis."

"Like, from under the ocean?" Cass said. "The whole island?"

"It's a Massa thing," I replied. "When Massarym stole the Loculi, raising the continent was part of his long-term plan. He wanted to bring back the glory that was Atlantis, blah-blah-blah."

Cass punched a fist in the air. "That is so emosewa!"

"Are you serious?" Aly leaned closer, all red in the face. "Um, tell me neither of you knuckleheads know what a disaster this would be."

"Right, tons of vromaskis and griffins and stuff," Cass said. "That would suck."

"No, that's not the point!" Aly said. "Millions of years ago, the entire middle of the United States was a sea. New York City had a mountain range like the Rockies. But the continents drifted. *Slowly.* Meteors collided, sea levels shifted, earth moved, air quality changed, continents sank, species died. *Incredibly slowly.* Raising an entire continent—*voom*, just like that? We're talking massive disaster. Tidal waves and earthquakes, to start. Changing wind and water currents, rising seas, coastal floods, shifting tectonic plates. New York City, Boston, Los Angeles, Seattle, Chicago, New Orleans, Athens, Capetown— gone. Don't even think about the Netherlands. Dormant fault lines burst open coast to coast, followed by fires. Dirt and dust clouds will block the sun, just like the time of the dinosaurs. And you know what happened to them. We'd be lucky if anyone survived!"

"Chicago's not coastal," Cass said.

"You get the idea!" Aly stared at me, her face a mixture

of fear and disbelief. "Do they really believe they can make the continent rise?"

"Maybe you're overreacting," I said. "How do you know it will be so bad? Maybe Atlantis isn't big enough to cause all that."

"It doesn't have to be that big to do a lot of damage, Jack!" Aly said.

"Well, people have been predicting ecological disasters and stuff anyway," I said. "At least this way, Atlantis would appear, with all its energy restored. And if the world had, like, good leaders, they could help."

Aly looked at me in disbelief. "How? Stop the floods with a proclamation?"

"They could think ahead," I said. "You know, evacuate people from the coasts. Look, we're already changing the climate by burning fossil fuels, right? And people are bombing and killing each other. There's genocide everywhere. It's not like the world is on a path to such a great future. Don't you think we *need* Atlantis?"

"I don't believe I'm hearing this," Aly said. "From Marco, yes. *He* thinks he's going to be king. But not from a reasonable, intelligent person like you. I say we kill this ridiculous discussion and stick to our plan. We contact the rebels, find out where the shards are hidden, get the other Loculi back, and kick some butt and figure out how to get off the island. That's going to be hard enough. Now, let's go to eat in the cafeteria, which probably *will* be bugged. Cass, if they drag you and me away to meet with Number One, we have to stay strong."

Cass giggled. "*Number One?* That's seriously her name?"

As she and Cass marched out the door, my head felt like it was whirling off my neck.

CHAPTER TWENTY-NINE
WHAT'S A FEW MILLION LIVES...?

I WAS GOING crazy.

I couldn't concentrate.

I thought about Aly's lecture on the great value of sleep. As she and Cass went off to the Comestibule—sorry, cafeteria—I tried to doze off. It didn't work. Being alone scared me.

So I got out of bed and trudged down to the cafeteria myself.

I found Cass downing powdered scrambled eggs as if they were about to go extinct. Old Mustafa the pilot was sitting at a table full of men, all laughing at some joke. Mrs. Petaloude sat a table all by herself with a plate full of bugs. Well, at least that was what it looked like. Aly was chatting up this skinny old scarecrow of a guy with a stiff gray beard that looked like it could scour pots.

"Jack!" she called out, waving me over. "Meet Professor Grolsch, the Most Interesting Man on the Island. He has like thirteen PhDs—"

"Phineas Grolsch," the old guy said, extending a bony hand, "and only two PhDs, plus an MA, MD, LLD, and MBA—Oxford, Cambridge, Yale."

"Um, Jack McKinley, Mortimer P. Reese Middle School," I squeaked.

"Cass Williams, starving," Cass said, bolting up from the table. "I'm getting seconds."

"We were discussing meteorological hypotheticals," Professor Grolsch said.

"Who?" I said.

Aly gave me a meaningful look. "You know, what would happen to the world if, say, I don't know, a *whole continent* was raised from the deep—"

"*Gro-o-olsch!*" Brother Dimitrios's voice snapped.

I spun around. Against the wall, at a long table, sat Dimitrios, Yiorgos, and the guy they called Cyclops, along with a bunch of sour-faced people in black robes. If eyes could kill, Professor Grolsch would be in the ground.

Grolsch's pale skin turned ashen. "Lovely to meet you," he said quickly and scooted back to his seat. "My oatmeal is getting cold."

Aly leaned close to me. "You see their reaction? They could tell what we were talking about. Grolsch was stalling. They *know*. About the destruction they're going to cause. But they don't care. What's a few million lives if they can rule the world?"

Out of the corner of my eye, I saw Brother Cyclops lumbering toward us. He nearly collided with Cass, who was carrying a plate of muffins, bacon, and doughnuts. "Sorry, you can't have any," Cass said, placing his tray at our table.

"Neither can you," Brother Cyclops said. "You have to meet someone."

"Wait—I—hey—!" Cass yelled as Cyclops pulled him toward the entrance.

Aly and I followed. At the front door, about ten Massa were gathered, busily chattering with someone in their midst. "Clear, please," Cyclops growled.

The crowd stepped aside, and Number One stepped through. She was dressed in layers of gossamer blue fabric embroidered with gold. As she lifted her hand, tiny jewels caught the morning sunlight. Neither Aly nor Cass shook the outstretched hand, so I did. "Guys, this is Number One."

Aly stared her square in the eye. "Do you have a real name?"

Number One threw back her head with a laugh. "I am so glad you asked. Yes, dear girl, my given name is Aliyah.

Come. We have much to talk about."

As the Massa turned back into the cafeteria, Number One turned the other way.

"*Number One* to you," Cyclops grumbled.

"And to you, too," Cass said.

Number One led us across the campus. Left and right, people stared in awe. I had the feeling she didn't appear in public very much. As she pointed out this and that new construction project, her voice was clipped and hurried. "As opposed to the Colonial-era foolishness of the Karai, we will have a facility light-years ahead of the technological curve," she said. "As Jack has seen, our security is quite comprehensive—and, trust me, he has not yet seen everything."

She gave me a sharp look and suddenly I was worried about our conversation outside the dorm. Had she heard us?

Easy. She's trying to rattle you.

We were headed toward the long brick building that was once the Karai Command Center. From behind it, I could see a cloud of dust. High-pitched voices rang out, yelling and laughing. But not Massa goon voices.

They were little-kid voices.

"What the—?" Aly said. "Your people bring their *kids* here?"

"Oh, great," Cass whispered, "we're going to be the Baby-sitters Club for the Massa nursery."

As Number One reached the back wall of the building, she turned. "I thought you'd like to see how we are preparing for a glorious future."

Behind the building, completely hidden from the campus, was a field of sparse grass that stretched at least fifty yards to an old barn. Fifteen or so kids were playing on it, arranged into groups with color-coded shirts. The oldest were about ten years old, the youngest around seven. Some were practicing jumps and headstands. A fire-hydrant-sized girl sprang past us doing backflips. Another girl was commanding a robot made from a dead stuffed monkey, making it walk in circles. Two others were racing up a huge tree, scaling it at impossible speed with only their hands.

"These aren't kids, they're freaks," Aly muttered under her breath.

Number One's eyes scanned the field. "Their teacher is supposed to be with them. . . ."

But I was looking toward a sudden commotion at the side of the field. There, three kids were reaching through a hole in a six-foot-high chain-link fence, taunting a pig using sticks and a cape, like matadors.

I stepped closer, and I realized it wasn't a pig.

"Is that . . . a *vromaski*?" I asked.

Number One's face stiffened. "They disabled the electrical protection. Children . . . children! *Where is your trainer?*"

She and I ran toward them, but the kids ignored her. As

one of them poked the vromaski, the bristles along its back stood on end. It swung around fiercely, spraying drool, its rubbery nose slapping against its own cheek. It eyed the attacker, a girl with dark skin and wild curly hair. She stuck out her tongue and did a mocking little dance. "Heeeere, piggy, piggy, piggy!" she called out.

"That kid is crazy," Cass said. "She's going to be killed!"

The vromaski coiled its hind legs and leaped up on to the side of the fence, grappling up the chain links with all four legs. It hauled its thick body upward before perching at the top, eyeing the dancing little girl. Its jaw dropped open, revealing a row of knife-sharp teeth.

Licking its lips, the vromaski leaped at its prey.

"Watch out!" I sprinted toward the girl, knocking her out of the beast's path.

Above me I heard a noise like a lion's roar crossed with a broken vacuum cleaner as the beast landed behind us. I scrambled to my feet. The vromaski turned and leaped again, its hairy ears swept back, a spray of drool flying from both sides of its mouth.

"No-o-o-o—"

Before I could move, its belly connected with my face.

CHAPTER THIRTY

ESIOLE

I FELL TO the ground. I struggled to keep my nostrils open, but the stench of the beast closed them back up again.

Pushing against the mud-encrusted belly of the beast was like trying to lift a subway car. It planted its clawed feet on the ground to either side of me, roaring, as it raised one tightly sinewed leg like a hawk after its prey.

Jamming my knees into the beast's underside, I rolled to the right and dug my teeth into the vromaski's other leg. It jerked away, its claws ripping a small hank of hair from my head.

I tasted blood. My mouth was on fire. I thought my tongue would shrivel up in my mouth. The spot where my hair had been ripped out felt as if someone had sliced it with a knife. The vromaski was jumping around now, letting out a sound between a squeal and a roar, pawing the ground wildly.

I sprang away from the slavering creature. It was surrounded now—kids with sharp sticks poking its sides, the curly-haired girl yanking on its neck with a lasso. Cass, Aly, and Number One ran over, grabbing the beast's collar, pulling it toward the pen.

"Trainer!" Number One cried out angrily.

Out of the corner of my eye, I spotted a pair of thick-muscled legs heading from the direction of the barn. A body hurtled toward the vromaski, colliding against its flank. The beast fell over, flailing its legs.

"Vromaski-tipping, my favorite pastime," a familiar voice said. "Wait till he farts. That's really fun."

I scrambled to my feet and caught a glimpse of my rescuer. The mop of shoulder-length hair was unmistakable. Not to mention shoulders as thick as a side of beef. His skin was tanned and his hair looked a shade lighter than I remembered, almost blond. His T-shirt and shorts were emblazoned with the Massa insignia, and an arsenal of weapons and instruments hung from his black leather belt.

He looked amazingly powerful, but you would expect that of a Select whose main talent was sports.

Aly's jaw was shaking as if the muscles were loose.

"Mar-*co*! Mar-*co*! Mar-*co*! Mar-*co*!!" the kids screamed.

204

The little girl, with a few quick motions, hog-tied the beast's feet together. "Ta-da!" she cried out.

Marco turned. "Good work," he said. "Okay, time to go home, Porky."

Grabbing the rope, he threw the squealing beast back into the pen.

"I did not just see that," Cass said.

Marco bounded toward us, a big smile on his face. "Heyyy, it's a Select reunion!"

I had never been so happy to see a traitor I hated so much. But what could I say to him? *Good to see you?* That wasn't true. So I settled for "Thanks, Marco."

"You know how much I hate vromaskis, Brother Jack." Marco held his arms wide. I think he expected us to rush toward him, but we didn't. Not even Aly.

Standing there a moment, he cast a nervous glance toward Number One. "So, you left your charges alone," she said.

"Yo, sorry, Numero Uno," he said. "I was teaching Gilbert to tie his shoes . . ."

"Ah, very important task indeed," Number One said dryly, "but important enough to put the rest of the trainees' lives at risk?"

"*I* lassoed it!" the curly-haired girl cried out. "It was *me*! Marco came out afterward!"

A group of boys giggled and began chanting, "Eloise,

smelloise, brain is made from Jelloise."

"*I'll lasso you, too!*" Eloise screamed, stepping toward the boys, who ran off giggling.

"Yo, little sister, *ssshhh*, put a lid on it," Marco said.

Eloise scowled at Marco. "Put a lid on your ugly face, Dumb Butt."

"My butt," Marco replied, "is actually pretty intelligent."

Number One glowered at him. "Then it compares favorably with your brain. Now go untie that beast, and *safely*. We need it for agility sessions."

Marco's cocky grin vanished. "Yes, ma'am."

As he turned and jogged back toward the pen, Eloise stomped away, back toward the big house.

"Just a moment, young lady," Number One said, following her.

Cass watched them go, shaking his head in awe. "She insulted him like that and all Marco could say was 'Yes, ma'am'?"

"He respects her," I said.

"He's afraid of her," Aly said. "Marco Ramsay is actually afraid of something."

Now Number One was returning with Eloise, whose arms were folded defiantly at her chest. "Eloise, dear, these are the other three of the Karai Select."

"So?" Eloise said.

"Well, you know how good Marco is at sports—Aly is

206

that good with computers," Number One replied.

Eloise put her hands on her hips. "Can you build one using strands of DNA to transmit data?"

"No one can do *that*!" Aly said with a laugh.

"Pffff," Eloise replied with an unimpressed shrug.

"And Cass is like a human gyroscope," Number One said. "Plus he can speak whole sentences backward."

"Iksamorv taht dekcor yllatot uoy, yeh!" Cass said.

Eloise rolled her eyes. "Gnirob yllatot."

Cass's eyes popped wide. "Cool, Esiole! You speak Backwardish?"

"Who can't?" Eloise retorted. "I stopped when I was seven. It's such a loser thing to do." She spun toward Number One. "Can I go now?"

With an exasperated sigh, Number One nodded. As Eloise went skipping away, Cass scowled. "Requesting permission to spank that little brat Eloise with a wooden elddap."

What was going on here? Who *was* this girl? Who were all of these freakish children?

In the vromaski pen, Marco and the other kids were hauling the beast through a gate. Outside the pen, other kids popped triple and quadruple midair spins.

"These are not normal kids," I said.

Number One managed a faint smile. "Unlike the Karai, we selected these children for G7W when they were very, very young. We thought with proper advance training, their bodies would become stronger, resistant to the gene's deadly effects."

I squinted my eyes, trying to make out the white lambda shape on the backs of their heads. "But they're too young to be Selects. None of them has the mark yet. How can you be sure?"

"A while back a brilliant geneticist joined our team," Number One said, "defecting from the Karai, by the way. Her technique revolutionized the diagnosis of G7W. With her genetic mapping analysis, we are now able to recognize the gene at birth. We no longer need to see the lambda."

I felt Aly's and Cass's eyes on me. We all knew a former Karai geneticist. I had spent my first seven years with her. "A while?" I said, trying to sound all la-di-da. "What's her name?"

"I believe you've met her," Number One said. "Sister Nancy."

I swallowed hard. How was this possible? My own mom, grooming Massa recruits? How could she do this?

Don't. Let. It. Show.

"Um, yeah, right, we did meet her, I think," I said. "But if she's from the Karai, how are you so sure you can trust her?"

"She came to us in a state of panic," Number One replied. "The Karai had placed a kill order on her. Because of a disagreement with your beloved Professor Bhegad."

"P. Beg?" Cass said. "He was disagreeable, but he wasn't a killer."

"Ah, but Professor Bhegad did not call the shots," Number One replied. "He followed whatever the Omphalos decreed. And when anyone crosses the Omphalos, they . . . disappear and never resurface. I would keep this in mind if you still harbor any crazy notions."

My head was about to explode. Seven lost years of my life finally made some horrible sense. Mom had disappeared because she had been afraid. Because her life had been on the line. "And . . . these kids," I said. "What will happen to them, now that we're here?"

"I suppose they will be our B team," Number One replied. "We don't have years to train them anymore. Your actions at the Heptakiklos changed everything, Jack. Our seismologists tell me the rip in the caldera of Mount Onyx is growing. If it bursts before the Loculi are returned, Atlantis will be lost forever."

"And if we return them," Aly said, "we raise an entire continent and destroy the world as we know it?"

"Evacuating coastal cities is difficult but possible," Number One said. "Losing Atlantis is a crime against humanity. But of course you wouldn't be here to see it, because if you don't return the Loculi, your time will have run out. Not to be cruel, but you'll be dead. So, children, it seems you have no choice but to join us. Can I count on you?"

Aly and Cass were staring at me. As if I were the only one who could sort this out. I averted my eyes, looking out across the vast field. Marco was nowhere to be seen.

Jack, you are the one who puts it all together. Professor Bhegad's words echoed loud in my brain.

We were losing sight of the plan. The plan was everything.

"Okay," I said. "We're with you."

"Jack!" Aly cried out.

"Under one condition," I added. "If you return the two Loculi to us, we will agree to reconstruct the third one."

Number One smiled patiently. "No conditions. We will construct it ourselves."

"You're not Select," I replied. "You can't."

"Let me ask you something, then, Jack," said Number One, stepping closer to me. "Haven't I been straightforward and honest with you?"

"I—I think so," I said.

"And you understand your own destiny on this island, don't you, Jack?" she asked.

Cass and Aly looked at me curiously. "Um, yeah . . ." I said.

"Then why on earth would you lie to my face right now?" she said.

My legs locked. *Lie?* Did she know about the plan? Or about Mom's identity?

"Wh-what do you mean?" I said.

"Earlier this morning, our Loculus shards went missing from their hiding place," Number One replied.

210

"Missing?" Cass squealed. "Who—?"

"Perhaps you can tell me," Number One said.

"Wait," Aly said. "You think *we* did that?"

"My dear, there are no other people on this island with any motivation." Number One held up her hand as if to stop us from protesting. "You're children. You do foolish things. I understand that. I will go away and let you return them, no questions asked. You have until nightfall."

"Or else what?" Cass said.

Number One turned to go. "There will be no 'or else.'"

211

CHAPTER THIRTY-ONE

THE KING OF TOAST

"YOUR OWN DESTINY on this island?" Aly was doing a great imitation of Number One's strange, faint accent. As she paced my dorm room, she ripped apart long strands of beef jerky, shoving the pieces into her mouth. "Don't tell me they're feeding you the same line they fed Marco."

My eyes strafed the room. Aly had disabled the spy cam, but I didn't trust the Massa. They might have had another one embedded in a cobweb or a speck of cockroach poop. I tried to catch her eye, to get her to be quiet, but Aly was on a roll.

"You're not answering me," she barged on. "Did they tell you you'd be king? Because you are King of Toast, Jack, unless you have some brilliant idea. Marco's turned into a camp counselor, your mom is a Massa recruiter, we're supposed to create global catastrophe—and just to make things more interesting, we were just accused of stealing the *only things that can save our lives*."

"Who could have stolen the shards?" Cass asked. "No one has any motivation!"

I eyed the iPod in a dock on my shelf. It was grubby and well used, probably stolen from a Karai worker, I figured. Quickly I flipped through the songs, mostly old pop tunes I would never listen to. Cranking it up, I hit shuffle and let her rip.

As the room echoed with sound, Aly covered her ears. *"Justin Bieber?"*

I walked right up next to her ear. "This place may be bugged," I said.

"But I—" she protested.

"They're smarter than you think," I said. "If we speak softer than the music, they won't hear us."

They both sidled closer.

"I think it's Fiddle," I whispered. "By taking the shards, the rebels may be sending us a signal. They know we're here and they want us to find them."

"Then why didn't they come for us directly?" Cass asked.

"We have been under constant surveillance," I said. "Finding the shards would be easier than reaching us."

"How do you figure that?" Aly asked.

"The rebels know this island," I said. "There must be at least one Karai security expert among them who can help them get past the Massa defenses and figure out where the likely hiding places are. So it's up to us to find the rebels."

"The last time we were here, when Fiddle liberated those Karai prisoners, he mentioned where he'd be taking them," Cass said. "He gave the location a name . . ."

"'*MO twenty-one—near Mount Onyx.*' That's what he said," Aly piped up.

A giant green bird flew past our window, disappearing into a tree bordering the jungle. Despite the brilliant tropical sunshine, the area beneath the tree canopies looked almost pitch-black. "We need to be careful, though. There are cameras in the jungle," I continued. "I don't know how many. We'll have to disable them."

"I can cross the signals," Aly said. "So one camera's feed will actually be another's. That way we'll pass by unnoticed."

"What if they track us?" Cass asked.

"I disabled our KI trackers," Aly reminded him.

"But they had some kind of tracking mechanism on us when I had to find you in the woods," I said.

Aly turned her shirt sleeve inside out and gave it a sharp tug. It ripped open, revealing a tiny, super-thin, wafer-like plastic chip. "That's why they made us wear these shirts," she said.

Cass and I quickly ripped out our chips and threw them

on the floor. I ran to the window and flung it open. It was a short drop to the ground and maybe a ten-yard run into the jungle. "Number One told us we had until darkness, 'no questions asked.' My feeling is they'll leave us alone. They'll see we ripped out the trackers but they'll think we're trying to cover up our hiding place. And they won't care where we hid the shards, so long as we bring them all back."

"What if we can't find the rebels by darkness?" Cass asked.

"The Massa need us," Aly said. "What could they possibly do?"

"They have a whole other team of Selects now," I reminded her. "I wouldn't count on kindness anymore."

I jumped out the window first. Together we raced into the jungle, leaving Justin Bieber far behind.

* * *

Within minutes, my shirt was sweat drenched.

We ran until we had to catch our breaths. I looked at my watch, and then upward into the deep green sameness. I could see the distant black peak of Mount Onyx above the tree line. "It's two thirty-seven," I said. "The sun sets around seven thirty."

"Hold it," Aly said. She pointed upward into the canopy of a tree. There, a small camera sat on a branch.

She quickly climbed to the branch, then pulled a nail file and a paper clip from her pocket. Prying open the back of the device, she tinkered with it and climbed down. "We're safe."

As if in response, an explosion of animal shrieks echoed back at us.

Cass jumped. "Who invited them?"

"They sound scared," I said. "Which means maybe we should be, too."

A sudden roar erupted from our right. The animal shrieks became panicked squeals. I could hear a thrashing of leaves not far away.

"Follow me!" Cass shouted. He raced away to the left. I grabbed Aly's arm and pulled her after him. There were no paths here, not even enough room for Aly and me to walk abreast. It took only a moment to lose Cass in tree cover. "Cass, where are you?" Aly cried out.

"Thirteen degrees southwest!" Cass yelled back.

"In human terms, please!" she shouted.

"Just follow my voice!"

I tried to keep up. My sandals caught on vines and roots. I whacked my head against a low-hanging branch. Visibility was about three feet, tops.

I lost sight of Cass first, and then Aly. "Guys?" I called out. *"Guys, don't get too far ahead of me!"*

No answer. The trees were so thick even sound didn't travel far.

By now I could smell the faint saltiness of sea air. That

meant we weren't too far from the beach. As I hauled myself around a fallen tree, I stopped to take a breath. A monkey swung overhead, and I felt a tiny nut bop the top of my head. "Thanks a lot," I grumbled.

Eeeee! cried the monkey. It was standing upright on a branch, gesturing deeper into the woods. *Eeee! Eeee!*

It looked a lot like Wilbur the extremely smart chimp, Torquin's friend, who had given his life for us. These island monkeys were not normal. This one seemed to be warning me.

"What?" I strained to see into the jungle but nothing seemed unusual.

Eeee!

"Thanks, that makes it clearer," I said.

There.

A flash of black.

I squinted. Something moved in the distance, from one tree to the next. As I instinctively jumped back, the monkey pounded its own chest as if to say *See? What did I tell you?* Then it swung away and out of sight.

"Hello?" I called out.

More than anything I wanted to hear Fiddle's voice or Nirvana's. But I got no response. I waited a few minutes, then picked up a rock and threw it in that direction.

With a hollow thump, it bounced off a tree and fell to the ground.

I looked back toward the direction Cass and Aly had

disappeared. They would be noticing my absence now. But if they tried to find me in these woods, they might get lost. Even with Cass's help.

"FI-I-I-DL-L-LE!" I shouted. Then, *"CA-A-A-ASSS! A-A-A-L-Y!"*

My voice echoed briefly into the canopies then faded quickly, answered only by a few curious bird calls. I began thrashing my way after Cass's path.

At least I hoped it was Cass's path.

The ocean smell came and went. I was sniffing up the sweat that poured down my face in torrents. Neither Cass nor Aly had left footprints in the thick piles of decaying leaves. My ankles were crosshatched with tiny lashes and swollen with bug bites. The trees seemed to be growing closer, threatening to strangle me. I knew it was the dead of afternoon, but the skies seemed to be darkening.

I heard a rustling sound and paused. *The sea?*

No. It was behind me. In the trees.

At the sharp, pistol-like snap of a branch, I spun around. The shape was closer, ducking behind a tree. I saw a flash of a black boot and knew it was human.

Not a rebel, I figured. They knew who I was, and they would come out of hiding to meet me. Then who? A Massa spy? "Hello? Hey, I see you. We were told we had until darkness!"

No response.

I turned and ran away as fast as I could. In about twenty yards I came to a dense copse off to the left and dived into the brush. My breaths came in loud, ragged gasps, but I tried to control the noise.

I heard footsteps. The figure was coming closer now. I could wait till he passed. Or jump him.

The steps crashed through the underbrush and then abruptly stopped. I held my breath. A mosquito buzz-bombed my ear and I swatted it.

Carefully I pushed aside the branches of the bush and peered into the pathway, where I'd last heard the steps.

It was empty.

I felt a hand grab my arm, and another jam against my mouth. A scream caught in my throat as I turned, staring into the fabric of a black hooded mask.

I struggled to get free. My attacker was trim and barely taller than me, but his strength was awesome. There aren't too many things more awkward than being dragged through a jungle by your arm. I stumbled in the brush and nearly fell three times.

He came to a stop near a fallen tree, set me against it, and whispered, "Speak softly."

It was not a *he* voice at all. I watched in disbelief as my assailant removed the black mask. My throat dried instantly, and I had to swallow to speak.

"Mom?"

CHAPTER THIRTY-TWO

REUNION

MOM'S HAIR WAS close-cropped, almost like a boy's haircut, but nothing could hide her humongous smile. "I am so, so sorry, Jack," she said softly, "but that place where I found you . . . it had cameras."

"It's o—" I said, but her arms were wrapped around me before I could get to the "kay."

I didn't think about cameras. Or about the island at all, or my body's time clock or the fact that my friends were nowhere to be seen. In that moment, seven years disappeared and I was a little kid again. I smelled mac and cheese bubbling on the stove, and a blast of chilly air through the kitchen door. I remembered the curve of her arms and her sweet smell and even her little, barely audible sob.

"I don't mean to smother you," she said. "I have been waiting to do this for years."

Smothering was okay. I gripped her as hard as I could. There was so much I wanted to say. A geyser of thoughts rose up inside me—angry and giddy, desperate and confused, all tripping over each other to get to my mouth. "How could you . . . why didn't you . . . Dad and me . . . all this time—"

"Shhhh," Mom said, placing her fingers on my lips. "Not so loud, Jack. There's so much I need to tell you. You're right to be upset. I never meant to abandon you and your dad, you have to know that."

"I do know," I said. "The Omphalos put a contract on your life. Number One told us."

"Yes," she said, tears gathering at the corners of her eyes. "I had no chance against him, Jack. If I hadn't carried out my plan in Antarctica, I would be dead now. And then I would have no chance to find a cure. No way to save you. I wanted to tell you and Dad, but it all happened so fast."

"But *why*?" I said. "Why would someone want to kill my mom?"

"Because I was hopelessly naive," Mom replied. "All I wanted was to find the cure, and I thought the Massa and Karai wanted that, too. But like the princes they were descended from, they couldn't agree. They worked in secret from one another, while kids all over the world were dying.

221

You were going to die. I decided to force them to work together. So when I began to unravel the G7W gene, I declared I'd give my findings to the Massa as well, so that our chances of finding a cure would be doubled. I asked the Omphalos to reach out to Aliyah. Instead, he ordered his people to kill me and take my work. I had no choice but to turn to the Massa. They took me in, no questions asked. They accepted my findings. Valued my work. But to be safe, I created a new identity so they wouldn't connect me to you."

I nodded. "So it's true. The Karai are the bad guys."

"No, no, it's not so simple." Mom shook her head, wiping her cheek. "You must understand, Jack, Professor Bhegad would never have wanted anyone to harm me. He was a mentor and a good, kind man, even if he didn't always show it. And I see now that the Omphalos only wanted to make sure the information didn't fall into the wrong hands. He saw that raising Atlantis would bring devastation. So their work is *good*, Jack."

"But their leader was ruthless . . ." I said.

"*Is*," Mom murmured.

She began to cry, and I couldn't help myself either. We both rocked back and forth in each other's arms. "I wish we could both go home," I said. "I wish we were all normal again."

Mom nodded, gently pulling back and looking me in

the eye. "We'll get through this, Jack. We'll get the Loculi and save your life. I swear it."

"Mom, Number One is threatening us," I said. "She thinks we stole the Massa's Loculus shards. But someone else did—"

I stopped short of mentioning the rebels. But Mom touched her finger to my lips, as if to shush me. "Of course you didn't. No one did. The shards are where they have always been since we got back to the island, in a secure hiding place very close to Aliyah."

"Wait. *What?*" I exclaimed. "So she lied to us? Why?"

"The same reason she lied about the xylokrikos and the electrified trap that wasn't."

Mom's raised eyebrow told a complete story. *Of course.* How could I have been so thickheaded?

"She's manipulating us," I said. "She knows we'd assume the rebels stole the shards. And that we'd go after them. So she's using us to flush them out of hiding. To do the work she can't do."

Mom nodded. "That is how the Massa work."

"Okay, we have to tell Cass and Aly," I said, looking over my shoulder. "Last I saw, they were headed to the beach."

Stiffening, Mom reached out and grabbed my arm. "Don't . . . move . . ." she whispered.

Directly ahead of us was a thrashing sound. Mom crouched behind the bush, pulling me with her. "With the

223

opening of the rift," she whispered, "there are all manner of beasts in the jungle."

"If it's a vromaski . . . ?" I said.

Mom gulped. "We run."

As we tensed for action, I heard another rustling noise— this time, behind us. I spun around in time to see Cass and Aly burst through the trees.

I put my fingers to my lips, and they fell silent. Mom was focused on the sound ahead of us, pointing a small gun. Through the trees emerged a massive figure with no hair; blackened skin; and filthy, ripped clothing. As his green eyes focused on us, Mom pulled her trigger.

"No!" screamed Aly. *Don't you know who that is?*

The giant attacker put a hand to his neck and fell to his knees. It was only by the sound of his roar and the scar on his cheek that I knew who he was.

PREPOSSEROUS

MOM TOOK AIM again, but I knocked the gun from her hand. *"Stop! You just shot Torquin!"*

As Aly ran toward the giant, Mom's mouth fell open. "But his face! I didn't recognize him."

"He was in an explosion," I said. "He—he should be dead."

"Now he is," Aly called out.

"No!" Mom said. "It's a tranquilizer bullet."

With a grunt, Torquin glanced at Aly, confusion dancing across his slitted eyes. His face was swollen and mottled with angry orange-red blotches. The lashes and brows had been scorched off. His unruly thick red mane was gone, leaving only a few ragged tufts of blackened hair.

225

I ran to him as fast as I could. Aly, Cass, and I tried to lift him to his feet, but it was no use. At nearly seven feet tall and three hundred pounds, Torquin was either going to fall or stand on his own.

Mom came toward us, frantically rummaging in a leather pouch. "He'll need an antidote. That dosage was enough to take down a rhinoceros."

"Pre . . . posserous," Torquin mumbled, his eyes crossing.

"Hold out his arm!" Mom pulled out a small vial and quickly yanked the cap off a hypodermic needle.

Torquin was swaying back and forth groggily, singing a song from *The Little Mermaid*. Lifting his arm was like trying to grab a tree trunk on a moving lumber truck. Mom broke three needles on his thick skin before she could administer the antidote. She sat with him, snapping her fingers in his eyes and slapping his cheeks to keep him awake.

In a moment Torquin's eyes fluttered. He lowered his chin and let out a belch that rocked his entire body.

"I think he's feeling better," Cass said.

Aly gave him a gentle hug. "I'm so glad you're alive."

I leaned close. "Torquin . . . it's Jack, Cass, and Aly. How did you survive that explosion?"

"Barely," Torquin grumbled, eyeing Mom warily.

"It's okay, she's on our side," I said. "She's my mom."

Torquin's eyes went from slits to saucers.

"I submit to no group," Mom said. "I am a free agent representing the interests of my son and the Select. I will keep your secrets and help you in any way."

"Saw explosion coming . . . ran . . . too late . . ." Torquin said. "Blew me into bushes. Woke up and walked to street, flagged taxi . . ."

"You got a taxi?" Cass said. "I wonder if it was the Massa spy?"

"No spy," Torquin said. "Driver saw me and ran away. Torquin drove cab to airport."

"So you got here with Slippy!" Aly said. "You slipped under the detection."

Torquin nodded, glancing around the woods. "And you found rebels?"

"Not yet," I said.

"They're here somewhere, Torquin," Mom said softly. "They operate at night with tiny acts of sabotage—setting fires, stealing food and equipment, disabling security. I don't know how they are surviving or how many there are. The Massa have not mounted a full-scale search for them yet, but it will happen soon, now that Dimitrios is back on the island. He suspects they're somewhere near Mount Onyx. But the place is surrounded by video feeds and nothing has ever been detected."

"We have to find them, Mom," I said. "And we have to get those shards. We have the missing piece, and it will fuse with the others. We can make that happen."

"The Massa have the Loculi of Invisibility and Flight, too," Aly said. "If we can get them, we'll have three."

"There's a fourth Loculus, too," Cass said warily, "but a god ran off with it. Long story."

"Can you get them for us, Mom?" I said. "The two Loculi and the shards of the third one? We need to get them and meet up with the rebels, and we have to do it all before darkness. If we're not back by then, they'll start coming for us."

Mom exhaled, looking back toward the compound. "It won't be easy. If they catch me, it will change everything. They will kill me."

"They can't catch you," I said. "Not after all these years, Mom. Promise me, please. Promise me they won't catch you?"

Mom met my glance levelly. She looked as if she'd aged just in the last few minutes. "I guess I need to make up for lost time, don't I? I promise, Jack. I have gotten very good at avoiding detection."

I nodded, but I felt as if someone had turned me inside out.

Torquin turned and blew his nose, sounding like the horn of an eighteen-wheeler.

"I will return to this spot as quickly as I can and give this signal—" Mom stuck two fingers into her mouth

228

and let out a raucous, three-note whistle. "Torquin, I will need you to come with me. There's one person I have to extract—someone the Massa may use as a hostage. She's a bit of a handful, but we can't leave her behind."

"Who is person?" Torquin said dubiously.

"Her name is Eloise," Mom said.

"What?" Aly blurted out.

Cass's face drained of color. "No. Absolutely not. Number one, she's disgusting. Number two, she's bratty. Number three, she's obnoxious and gross—"

"Number four, Cass," Mom said with a sigh, "she's your sister."

CHAPTER THIRTY-FOUR
MY SISTER THE MONSTER

AFTER CASS FINISHED cackling, he picked himself off the ground and wiped off clumps of jungle leaves. "Oh, thanks," he said. "That is hilarious. I like your mom, Jack. She doesn't take life too seriously, even at times like this. *My sister! Ha!*"

Mom's expression was dead steady. "Cass, I need your cooperation on this."

A laugh caught in Cass's throat. "Hrm. So you—I mean, this is a—you can't . . . um, Mrs. McKinley, you don't know me, but I can assure you I don't have a sister. I'm an only child."

"And I'm a geneticist," Mom said. "Your parents gave birth to a girl when you were four years old. At the time, you were in foster care. Like you, she became a ward of the state."

Cass nodded. "I was with the Hendersons."

"They called you Li'l Runt," Mom said. "You slept in a room by the laundry machine. There were four other children."

"You didn't have to remind me of that," Cass said.

"G7W runs in families, Cass," Mom said. "It's not so surprising she has it."

"She does look like you," Aly volunteered.

"She speaks Backwardish," I added.

Cass put his head in his hands. "Won em toohs."

* * *

As we walked toward Mount Onyx in search of the rebels, my head throbbed and my ankles looked like the surface of a pizza. I felt like we'd walked into a flash mob of mosquitoes. I'd slapped my own face so much I nearly dislocated my jaw. Above us a team of monkeys took turns dropping nuts on us and screeching with hilarity.

"Ow!" Cass flinched. "Why is it they always seem to hit *me*?"

"Shhh," Aly said. "We have to hear Jack's mom's whistle."

"Tell that to the monkeys!" Cass said.

I looked at my watch. 4:43. "We have to be patient."

"Right. She and Torquin have to deal with my sister the monster," Cass said, as another fistful of nuts rained around him. "Maybe she's actually up there with her look-alikes."

A high-pitched whine sounded in the distance, and we stopped. It grew louder like a police siren. "An alarm," Aly said. "Your mom mentioned there were—"

She was interrupted by the crack of a gunshot. Shrieking, the monkeys almost instantly disappeared.

"Th-that was from the direction of the compound," Cass said.

The blood rushed from my head. *If they catch me, it will change everything,* Mom had said. *They will kill me.*

I began running toward the noise. "Mom!"

"Jack, what are you doing?" Aly shouted. "Come back here!"

I ignored her, racing through the jungle. My bug-swollen ankles scraped against thorns and branches. The sun was beginning to set below the tops of the trees, darkening the path. In a moment I could hear Cass and Aly running behind me, shouting.

Another shot rang out. I was off course. Too far to the north. As I shifted my path, I could hear a thrashing in the woods.

A shrill, three-note whistle pierced the air.

Mom.

"Over here!" I bellowed.

A shadow materialized between two trees, and in a moment, I saw Mom's face. At first it looked like she was wearing a half mask, like the Phantom of the Opera, but when I got close I realized the left side of her face was coated with blood. *"Mom! What happened?"*

She held up her left hand, which was wrapped in a bloody towel. "The safe . . . was booby-trapped," she said, gulping for breath. "My hand got stuck . . . I wiped it on my cheek. Face is fine, but the hand will need some TLC. I'll be okay, Jack."

"Did they see you?" Cass asked.

"I don't think so," Mom replied. "I wore gloves. No prints. But I can't be sure."

As Cass and Aly ran up behind me, I realized Mom had a giant sack slung over her shoulder. She swung it around, letting it thump heavily on the ground. "There are three steel boxes inside," she said, "with the two Loculi and the shards. Each box is secured with an encrypted electronic lock. We will have to worry about that later."

"You're the best, Mom," I said. "But I'm worried about you."

"Don't be," she said. "You guys don't have the time to—"

YEEAAAAARRGHH!

A roar like an angry lion blasted through the jungle. As we all spun toward it, a different voice wailed, high-pitched and nasal: *"Ew, ew, ew, ew, ew—that tastes disgusting!"*

Torquin crashed through the underbrush, stepping into the clearing. His browless eyes were scrunched with pain and even in the dim light I could see a crescent-shaped red mark on his right arm. Yanking his arm forward, he dragged Eloise into sight. "She bit me," he said.

Cass looked at Mom's belt pouches. "You have a rabies shot in there, by any chance?"

"*Rrrrrraaachhh, ptui!* When was the last time you took a bath, Hulk?" As Eloise spotted Mom, then us, the agony on her face vanished. "Sister Nancy? What's going on?"

Mom took Eloise by the arm and brought her forward. "Eloise, dear, come meet your brother."

"I don't have a brother," she said.

"Sweetheart, you do," Mom said. "This is Cass."

Eloise's face fell. "The dorky one?"

Cass waggled his fingers. "Sorry."

"I feel sick all over again," Eloise said.

"Well, that's a touching reunion," Aly said.

Mom knelt by Cass's sister, looking her in the eye. "Eloise, the Massa took you from your foster home and told you a lot of things—"

"They said *you* picked me!" Eloise replied. "They told me I had no mom and dad."

Mom nodded sadly. "The Massa have forced both of us to do things we never should have done. They are keeping many truths from you. Before they brought you here, they did some horrible things to the Karai Institute, the people who first settled this place."

"Those were the rebels, the bad guys . . ." Realization

flashed across Eloise's face. "Sister Nancy . . . you're a spy?"

"Do you trust me, Eloise?" Mom asked.

"Yes! You're—you're amazing," Eloise replied. "You're the only one who's nice to me, but—"

"Do you believe I'm telling you the truth?" Mom pressed. Eloise nodded silently.

"It's a long story, dear," Mom said, "and there will be time to tell it someday soon. Jack is my son. I was forced to leave him, too. Please, stay with him and your brother. These people have your best interests at heart. Not the Massa."

Eloise stared at her feet for a few seconds. Cass moved toward her. He looked like he wanted to put his arm around her, but finally he just stood by her side.

When Eloise spoke, her voice was barely audible. "Okay," she said. "I believe you, Sister Nancy. But—I did something really dumb." She glanced up at Torquin. "When this guy came to take me, I set off the alarms all by myself."

"Wait—*you* set those off?" Mom said.

"I'm sorry!" Eloise looked like she was going to cry.

"No, no, that's all right, dear," Mom said.

She looked at me, and I knew exactly what she was thinking. If the alarms hadn't been tripped by Mom—if they were focused on another area of the compound—then maybe she hadn't been seen after all. A smile flashed across her face. "I can't hang around. But promise me you'll stay with your brother?"

"Where will you go, Sister Nancy?" Eloise asked.

"Back to the Massa. But I'll be watching, from a safe place," Mom replied. "As much as I can."

The words hit me hard. "Come with us, Mom."

"I—I wish I could," Mom said. "But the Omphalos does not forget or forgive. If I joined you I wouldn't last long, Jack. As for the Massa . . ." She let out a long sigh. "I'm hoping they don't suspect me. If they do, I'll need to go into hiding."

"No!" I blurted out. My face was boiling hot. I could barely see Mom through a surge of tears, as if she were already beginning another slow fade into memory.

She touched my chin with her bandaged hand. "You're beginning to look so much like your father."

"He misses you, too, Mom," I said. "A lot. Just as much as I do. What if we never see each other again? If the Massa catch you . . . or the continent is raised and floods the coasts? What happens if I turn fourteen before—"

Mom wrapped me in a hug and whispered into my ear. "I failed you, Jack. I was going to find the cure, but I didn't. Now it's your turn. You'll have to figure it out. You and your friends are the only ones who can. Take care of the Loculi."

With that, she released me and ran off into the jungle.

I watched as the darkness swallowed her up.

CHAPTER THIRTY-FIVE

GOON NUMBER SEVEN

MY WATCH CLICKED from 6:36 to 6:37.

The jungle was nearly dark. We could just barely see the contours of the trees. I'd strapped my flashlight to my head. Cass was in front, but the going had been slow. Right now we were standing still in a clearing, waiting for Aly to rewire a camera in a tree. It was the fifth one she'd found.

"Can't you do that faster?" Cass hissed.

"Done," Aly said, hopping down. "Next time *you* do it, Mr. Jitters."

"Did you just call me *Mr. Jitters*?" Cass shot back. "This isn't a stroll in the woods, Aly. They told us we had till darkness. Look up!"

"Cass, the sun hasn't completely set yet," I said. "It just

looks dark because we're in a jungle! Aly's trying to keep us safe."

Cass took a deep breath. "Right . . ." he said, turning back toward the mountain. "Right . . ."

"Are you sure we're related?" Eloise asked.

We began trudging again. With each step, the sack of Loculi grew heavier and heavier around my shoulder. "Guys, I really need to rest," I said.

"No!" said Cass.

"Yes!" said Eloise and Aly at the same time.

I stopped walking and let the sack drop. Eloise sighed deeply, leaning against a tree. I looked back into the blackness, expecting Torquin to lumber up to us, but he wasn't there. "You okay, Tork?" I called out.

Cass came up beside me. "Maybe he caught a vromaski in his bare hands and decided to eat it."

"*Torquin!*" I shouted, walking back the way we came, shining my flashlight around.

"Yo, Tork!" Aly said.

As we reached the clearing where Aly had rewired the last camera, I stopped.

My flashlight focused on a massive lump at the edge of the clearing—Torquin, lying on his side with his eyes closed and mouth wide open.

"Is he sleeping?" Eloise asked.

I raced toward him and knelt by his side. His chest was

moving. I grabbed his shoulders and tried to shake him. "Torquin!" I said. "Get up! We're almost there!"

"That's good to know," came a voice from the darkness.

Eloise screamed. I stood up quickly, my flashlight tracing the contour of a long black robe until it reached the bearded face of Brother Dimitrios.

"That's a bit bright," he said, shielding his eyes with a hand that was clutching a truncheon. "But alas, your overgrown Karai thug is not. Although I give him credit for getting here. We certainly didn't expect to find him."

"You cheated!" Eloise said. "You told them you were going to come in darkness. Liars!"

Dimitrios's eyes widened. "That was before you tripped off the alarms, young lady. Oh, yes, we saw that. That is your gratitude for all we've done? You connive with these hoodlums to steal the two Loculi and the Loculus shards, and then try to take them to the rebels? I'm sorry, children, this game is over. We can no longer trust you."

"Oh blah-blah, fumfy-fumf, look at me, I am soooo important." Eloise folded her arms.

"Trust *us*?" I said. "You were the ones who lied. You accused us of stealing the shards when you were really hiding them. You were using us—trying to get us to flush out the rebels!"

"I must say I admire your cleverness and your cheek," Dimitrios said, rubbing his forehead. "I don't know how you discovered our little plan, much less how you found the shards' location. But I'm disappointed that you needed to twist young Eloise's impressionable mind, convincing her to do your dirty work—"

"I can think for myself, Brother Dimhead," Eloise said. "Leave us alone."

"I was given clear instructions, princess—shards, Loculi, and Select. Immediately. Number One would like to talk to you." Brother Dimitrios exhaled, looking down at Torquin. "By the ghost of Massarym, she will not be pleased to see this one."

I glanced nervously back into the jungle. The Loculi and the shards were sitting in my backpack, just beyond the clearing. I couldn't see the backpack now, but it would be easy to find. We had to get rid of this guy. "Sorry, Brother D," I said. "We don't have the Loculi and the shards. And we won't tell you where they are. So *you* go back and tell that to Number One."

"Yeah!" Eloise said, sticking out her chin.

"I don't believe I offered no as an option." Brother Dimitrios reached into his pocket and took out a gun.

"He's going to shoot me?" Eloise said.

"Over my dead body," Cass said, stepping in front of her. Then he flinched. "Oh wow, did I really just say that?"

Brother Dimitrios snapped his fingers. Behind him, out of the shadows, stepped a team of Massa—Cyclops, Yiorgos, Mustafa, and two others I didn't recognize. "You know most of these gentlemen," Dimitrios said. "May I introduce two of our most accomplished security staff, Mr. Christos and Mr. Yianni."

Christos had the build of a sumo wrestler and Yianni looked like he'd stepped off the Russian Olympic basketball team. Mustafa was flexing his arms, and the bruises from the minivan window looked like dancing tattoos.

"There are *six* of you?" Aly said.

"Actually, seven," Dimitrios said, glancing over his shoulder for his missing goon. "Like the Loculi."

"And the Wonders," Yiorgos said. "It is a lucky number."

Now I could make out a seventh massive silhouette behind the rest, his face shielded by a hood. This group was practically a squadron.

And our plan was dead.

Dimitrios's goons fanned out on either side of him, as if to impress us—first Mustafa, then Yiorgos and Cyclops, and then the two new guys.

"Any more protests, children? Good. Now, let's move quickly. We need to get Mr. Torquin to our hospital." Dimitrios pointed to the hooded goon. "You will keep Jack company while he fetches the Loculi. Move!"

The seventh Massa stepped forward. As I turned to him, my flashlight beamed smack into his eyes.

He flinched away, but not before I got a clear view of Marco Ramsay.

CHAPTER THIRTY-SIX
PULL MY FINGER

ALY LUNGED FORWARD and slapped him.

"Ow!" Marco said.

"*Et tu*, Marco?" she said through gritted teeth.

"Dude, I didn't study French," Marco said. "Look, no one told me Brother D was packing. I thought I was just coming to pick you guys up."

"It happens to be Latin," Aly said, "and it means, 'And you?' From *Julius Caesar*—who said it to his trusted friend Brutus right before Brutus stabbed him."

Marco grinned. "You and old movies. Dang. Gotta rent that one. But listen, Als, I'm not like that—"

"You two may continue your love spat at another time," Brother Dimitrios snapped. "Marco is a soldier,

242

and a soldier takes orders."

"I can't believe this," Cass said. "That's what *Soldier* means to you now, Marco? If Dimitrios told you to kill us, would you do that? Or maybe trap the rebels and bring them back to be tortured—your *friends*? Huh?"

"You're delaying us, Cass," Dimitrios said. "We have no incentive to harm these rebels. We shall restore them to health. Reason with them. Make them see that our interests are the same—"

"How's that working with the group we saw *in chains*?" Cass's face was red. Veins bulged from his neck as he walked straight up to Marco. "How does it feel to be a soldier for *liars and murderers*?"

"Dude, whoa," Marco said. "The pharmacy here has some good herbal anxiety remedies—"

"And the way you talk is idiotic," Cass spat back. "What happened to that promise to make you Massa king? You're a Massa nanny! A punching bag for little rug rats. What happens when you finally have an episode—or do you still think you're immortal?"

Mustafa lumbered forward. "Let me take care of that one."

"Chill, Moose Taffy," Marco said, then turned back to Cass. "Dude, I *had* an episode. They thought I was going to die. But the scientists here? They're off the charts, Brother Cass. One of them brought out the shards. He figured he

243

would put the Loculus of Healing together for me. He couldn't, but just being near those suckers—they made me feel better." He smiled. "They saved my life. And they'll do the same for you. So give Brother D a chance, dude!"

"Aaaaauuuurrrrrgh!" With a scream that seemed to come from somewhere in Cass's solar plexus, he ran for Marco at full tilt.

Marco's eyes shot open wide with shock. Cass swung at his face with the flashlight, but Marco caught his arm easily. "Easy, little brother," Marco said with a baffled laugh.

Cass spun around, ducked, and head-butted Marco in the belly. Marco staggered backward, more surprised than hurt.

"Seize him!" Brother Dimitrios cried out.

"I HATE YOUUUUUU . . ." Cass's voice was a distorted scream. He was in an out-of-control windmilling frenzy, all arms and legs, like some berserker at a mosh pit. He clipped Brother Yiorgos in the eye with a flying finger and kicked Brother Christos in the groin.

Or maybe it was Brother Yianni.

Christos-or-Yianni folded, groaning. But the other four Massa moved fast, surrounding Cass. Aly and I tried to pull them away, but their backs were like a thick wall. In about two seconds, we could no longer see Cass's whirling-dervish arms. In about three, we stopped hearing his voice.

"Get away from him!" Aly shouted, finally managing to

plow through the Massa guards.

In the center, Cass was crumpled up in the dirt.

"Nerve pinch in the neck," Brother Yiorgos said. "Painless. He will be fine."

"I could finish the job," Mustafa said.

Dimitrios scowled at him. "We are not barbarians."

"Could have fooled me," said Eloise, kneeling by her brother.

"Whoa, me, too, little sister." Marco stepped forward, then fell to his knees next to Eloise. He reached down to Cass, straightening out his head, which had become twisted to the side. "That was pretty harsh, Brother D."

"It is a pity that he attacked us," Dimitrios said.

Marco turned to him. "Dude, did you ever think—hey, is this any way to treat one of our future bosses?" he said. "Because you know Brother Cass is going to be pretty powerful in the kingdom of His Jackness."

He glanced over to me and flipped a thumbs-up.

I gulped. He knew about the prophecy!

"Jack . . ." Aly said. "What is he talking about?"

"You don't know?" Marco said, as he sat Cass up against a tree. "Old Jacko is going to be our king—not me, like they first thought. Seventh Prophecy says it's a win for McKinley!"

Eloise's face lit up. "Does he get a crown?"

"A big one, with jewels, I hope," Marco said.

"So that's why Dimitrios was acting nice to us all along." Aly shot me a sharp, assessing glance. "And it's why he pulled Jack away from us, yesterday morning . . ."

"Hey, maybe you also noticed how he was treating your pal Marco?" Marco said. "One minute a hero, the next—*bam!*—a slave. Because that's that way Dimo rolls: butter up the superiors, spit on everyone else. So I gotta say, D, the boss lady's not going to be happy about the way you're treating Jacko the Future King. In the new world order, you're gonna be like a sewer inspector. Or a vromaski catcher."

"We have no time for chatting," Brother Dimitrios barked. "All of you—take Torquin and the boy, and let's go!"

From below, Cass groaned in pain. As his eyes fluttered open, Marco knelt over him. "Good morning."

Cass hocked a glob of spit into Marco's face. *"Traitor!"*

"Auuuccchh, did you have to do that?" Marco said, staggering backward.

Christos reached down and grabbed Cass's arm. "Get up."

"Leave him alone!" Eloise shouted, kicking the goon in the shin.

Yianni grabbed the back of her T-shirt and lifted her high. "Little mosquito," he said with a grin.

With superquick reflexes, Marco snatched her away and set her down gently. He turned to Yianni and stuck a finger in his chest. "Back off, baklava breath."

"Marco . . ." Brother Dimitrios growled. "Remember whose side you're on."

"Yeah, didn't mean to diss you, Yianni, your breath is more like moussaka. With extra garlic. Peace out." He stuck out his hand toward the Massa goon. With a reluctant grunt, Yianni reached out to shake it—but Marco yanked back his hand, holding up one finger. "Pull my finger."

Yianni looked at him, slack-jawed.

"Do I need to speak Greek?" Marco said. "Pullus fingeropoulos. Aly? Cass? Dimitrios? Christos? Yiorgos?"

"*HAW!*" Brother Cyclops broke into a deep belly laugh. "I love this kind of joking!"

"Jack?" Marco said. "Et tu?"

"*Have you all lost your minds? Let's go!*"

Dimitrios was shouting, but the other men were hesitating. Marco may have been demoted, but those goons knew what he could do, and they were afraid.

I wasn't. Marco was holding up his finger to me, a crazy look in his eye. And I was in no mood for games.

"Sorry, Marco," I said. "No."

Marco looked chagrined. "No? Do you know what that means, Brother Jack? How about you, Brother D? *Do you know what this means?*"

"Number One will get a report on each of you if you don't act now!" Dimitrios snapped his fingers, and the other five goons all stepped toward Marco.

"It means . . . *escape valve not activated*." Marco began spinning around wildly, finger in the air. "Aaaaaahhhhh!"

"*Grab him!*" Brother Dimitrios shouted.

"*Losing controlllllll!*" Marco took one step toward Cyclops, leaped high, and landed a kick on the man's jaw. The big man jolted back and fell to the ground in a heap.

Dimitrios lifted his gun to Marco's face.

"Don't!" Aly screamed.

Marco crouched into a football stance. "Brother D, I have wanted to do this for a long time."

Dimitrios pulled the trigger. The bullet winged over Marco as he hit the monk headfirst with a flying tackle, driving him into a tree. With a helpless cry, Dimitrios lost consciousness and crumpled to the ground.

Marco sprang to his feet as the other Massa rushed toward him.

"*Don't just stand there, Jack!*" Marco shouted. "Be a king!"

CHAPTER THIRTY-SEVEN

THE MEATHEAD STARTS OVER

NO TIME TO think. I leaped toward Brother Yiorgos's legs and tackled him to the ground. His head hit the side of a tree with a thud.

Aly was right behind me. She'd grabbed my backpack from the shadows and removed the sack containing the three boxes full of Loculi. With a grunt, she swung them at Brother Christos. He tried to duck, but she connected squarely with the side of his head, and he collapsed in pain.

"Kcatta!" Cass jumped onto Christos's back. The goon straightened up and twirled him like a backpack.

"I'll take over from here," Marco said, lifting Cass away. As Christos faced him, Marco took him out with an upper-cut to the jaw. "Three down. Two to—"

As he turned to me, a pair of hands reached around and grabbed my throat. Marco darted toward me but stopped short as Brother Yianni pulled out a knife and held it to my throat. "Party over," he growled into my ear.

Marco, Cass, and Aly stood paralyzed, staring at me in dismay, their breaths coming in gulps.

"Let him go, Yianni," Marco said.

"Where is Mustafa?" the man replied.

"He was here a minute ago," Marco said, his eyes darting from side to side.

Christos tightened his grip. *Mustafa! Where are you?*

At the edge of the clearing, a tall, rangy silhouette staggered forward. "Here," Mustafa said, barely audible.

As he got closer, it was clear that his eyes were closed, his head lolling to one side. "Acchhh, *vre*, Mustafa, drinking *now?*" Yianni said with disgust.

As Mustafa slouched forward, I could see a set of thick fingers gripping either side of him, holding him upright from behind.

He stopped moving and fell to the ground in a limp heap. Torquin, burned and smiling, stood over him. "Surprise."

It was all the distraction I needed. I shoved my elbow back into Yianni's midsection. As he let out a grunt of surprise, his hands loosened around my neck.

I dropped to the ground and rolled away. Marco and

Torquin were running toward me, but there wouldn't be enough time. Yianni whipped his arm around, the knife slashing through the air toward my face. All I could think to do was kick his knee. Hard.

With a scream, Yianni fell back. The knife flew out of his hand. Before he hit the ground, Marco was on top of him, delivering a punch to the face.

As he went still, the jungle was quiet again. Even the birds seemed to have backed off.

Marco stood up, wiping his brow. "I could go for some ice cream."

Cass was staring at him in awe. "That was gnizama."

"And soooo scary!" Aly cried out, nearly tackling me with a hug.

It hurt. My whole body hurt. But I didn't push her away. Somehow the pain was, for that moment, tolerable.

Torquin was stepping toward Marco, clenching and unclenching his fists. His face, already burned, was turning redder.

"Whoa, is that Torko the Terrifying?" Marco exclaimed. "Dude, nice haircut!"

"Torquin clobber Marco the Meathead," the big guy growled.

"*No,*" I said. "Leave him, Torquin! He saved us. He did . . . all this."

Torquin looked around at the unconscious Massa.

"But—Marco is—"

We were all looking at Marco now. "Explain yourself," Aly said softly. "Because right now, to me, you are a big enigma."

Marco scratched his head. "I'm a ship?"

"*Enigma* means 'mystery,'" Aly said with a groan. "Herman Wenders just gave that name to his ship!"

"Marco, why did you turn on the Massa like that?" I asked.

Marco shrugged. "You didn't pull my finger."

"Not funny." Torquin lunged at Marco, grabbing his tunic collar and raising a fist. "I have message. From Professor Bhegad."

"Whoa, back off, Kong! Chill," Marco said, wriggling loose from Torquin's grip. "No more joking. I promise. Look, I messed up. Totally. I've been thinking about this a lot. I mean, okay, back at the beginning? Brother D is all, behold His Highness Marco the Magnificent, woo-hoo! At first I'm skeptical, because I don't want to leave you guys— but they're all, hey, no worries, your pals will come over. So I listen to their side of the story and it makes sense. Plus, I get to fight beasts and learn leaps and other stuff while I'm waiting for you guys to change your mind and go Massa."

"You really thought we'd do that?" Aly asked.

Marco nodded. "I hoped you would. They treated me really well. Until one day it's like, *meeeeeaaaaah*, you missed the daily double, sorry, we changed our minds. I start having to train these bratty kids and people are ordering me around like I'm just another goon. No one says why, so I start really listening to their conversations and they're all about raising the continent, and death counts, and body disposals—and suddenly Brother D is talking about the *Destroyer* and *Loculus shards*, and I'm like *what?* Then one day, bang, you guys are here. No warning, nothing. I see how they're treating Jack, and I start putting two and two together— but slowly, because math is not my strong point . . ."

His voice trailed off. I didn't recognize the expression on his face, because I'd never seen it before.

I was guessing vulnerability.

Aly stepped closer to him, but he turned away. "So, yeah," he said. "I was a traitor. You guys can be haters, I understand that. But it's over with the Massa and me. Sorry for being such a dork. You, too, Tork." A tiny smile grew across his face. "Traitor, hater. Dork, Tork. I'm a poet and I don't know it."

Torquin turned to us. "This is English?"

"I understood it," Aly said. She reached out and put a hand on Marco's arm. "I want to believe you. But you really hurt us, Marco. How can we trust you?"

"Don't you?" Marco swallowed. "I mean, we're family, remember?"

No one answered.

"Professor Bhegad always said trust had to be earned," I said quietly.

Marco nodded. He looked us each in the eye. I was afraid he'd make some lame joke, but he looked more serious than I'd ever seen him. "So I guess I start now."

He reached out with open arms. Eloise, who had been standing silently the whole time, flew into them. He lifted her off the ground.

Aly was next, then Cass, and finally I gave in, too. He lifted us all, and it felt really good to have him back.

"Marco, I'm curious about one thing," I said as he let us down. "What would you have done if I *had* pulled your finger?"

"Farted," Marco said.

Aly grimaced. "Maybe we don't want you back."

But Marco didn't answer. His eyes were focused into the woods, and he swallowed hard. "Dudes," he whispered, "they're coming in quick. We are toast unless we move now."

"You can see that?" Cass said.

"A night-vision thing," Marco said. "G7W works in mysterious ways. Get down! Now! *DOWN!*"

We all hit the ground. I heard whistling noises, followed by thuds.

A few feet away, Brother Yianni's body jerked, an arrow jutting up from him.

CHAPTER THIRTY-EIGHT

AMBUSH

ARROWS WHISTLED PAST us. A monkey fell from a tree with an agonized howl. I ducked behind Brother Dimitrios's motionless body. The sack that contained the Loculi was just to my left, lying next to my backpack. I gathered them both up and held them close.

Aly stared at the arrow stuck in Yianni's chest. "They're hitting their own people!"

"What do we do now, your majesty?" Marco called out.

Don't run if you don't know where the enemy is.

I took a deep breath and fought back panic. I didn't want to lead us into ambush. Peering up from behind Brother Dimitrios, I watched the arcs of the arrows as they dropped into the clearing—all from one place, directly opposite us.

Cass was the one who could guide us to the volcano. But he was still shaking. I was worried about him. We would need him to focus on his own skills, but he was a basket case right now.

I grabbed a knife, a gun, and a flashlight from the belt of Brother Dimitrios. "They're all clumped together," I said. "We need to get out of the arrows' pathway. It's dark, but I think I can get us clear. Cass, when I give the word, can you put us back on the path to Mount Onyx?"

"Yeah, but—" Cass said.

"Good!" I shot back. "Follow me! *Now!*"

I hooked the backpack over my shoulder. Crouching as low as I could, I ran. I used my flashlight to guide the way in the darkness and Dimitrios's knife to bushwhack a path through the vines and branches.

I was nearly out of breath when the trees gave way to a swamp. I paused by the edge. My flashlight beam was starting to dim and I shut it off. The only sounds I could hear now were my own breaths and the buzz of mosquitoes hovering over the muck. "Hold up!" I said, as Aly, Marco, and Torquin ran up beside me.

I waited for two other sets of footsteps.

"Um, where's Cass?" I said.

A distant, high-pitched shriek was my answer. *"Eloise!"* Aly said. "Something happened to her."

She and I jumped toward the sound, but Torquin

grabbed both our arms. "Getting Cass not safe."

"Leaving Cass not sane," Marco said, sprinting into the jungle.

"Don't!" Aly cried out, but he was out of sight.

As Torquin roared his disapproval, I pulled loose of the big guy's grip.

"Don't you dare go after them and leave me alone," Aly said.

"I have a gun," I said. "If we circle around carefully, we can surprise the attackers."

"You're going to *shoot* them?" Aly said. "When have you ever shot anything?"

"I went duck hunting with my dad," I said. "Once."

"Did you hit any of them?" she asked.

"I missed on purpose," I said. "Come on!"

Without waiting for a reply, I dropped the backpack on the ground, flicked on my flashlight, and began to run. I beat a path parallel to the one we'd taken, keeping Eloise's screams to my left. The attackers would be following her screams, too. If they got to her first, we needed to be in a position to ambush.

At the distant sound of rumbling voices, I stopped. Aly and Torquin came up behind me. I put my finger to my lips and clicked off the flashlight.

The attackers were directly ahead. I heard a moan, and some frantic-sounding whispers. As we tiptoed closer, branches cracked beneath our feet, but no one seemed to hear us.

There.

About twenty yards in front of us, a dim light flickered. I fell to my chest and crawled forward, until I could make out a group of silhouettes gathered around a fire— not many, maybe three or four. As Aly and Torquin crawled up beside me, I took aim with the gun. My hands shook.

"What are you doing?" Aly said. "What if you hit Eloise or Cass?"

"I don't see them," I said.

"Time to squash Massa," Torquin said, crouching as if to pounce.

The voices fell silent. Torquin fell to his stomach, and we all held our breath.

A moment later, I heard the click of a cocked pistol from behind us.

Aly smacked my arm. "Stop it. This king stuff is going to your head."

"It wasn't me!" I protested.

"What?" Aly shot back. "Then who—?"

I whirled around, gun in hand.

"Drop it, cowboy," a female voice said.

I let the gun fall. Rising to my knees, I put my hands in the air. Together, Aly, Torquin, and I stood and turned.

A dark figure stood before us, holding a flashlight. Slowly she pointed it toward herself, chest high, shining it upward until her own face was revealed.

"Why didn't you lame-os tell us it was you?" said Nirvana.

CHAPTER THIRTY-NINE

FIDDLE AND BONES

THE BLACK LIPSTICK was gone.

That was the first thing I noticed. Her jet-black hair was growing in sandy blond, her cheekbones were sharper, and her skin was deeply tanned. But there was no mistaking Nirvana's lopsided, ironic smile. "You . . . scared me . . ." was all I could think to say.

"Be glad I'm not wearing my goth makeup. You'd have a heart attack." She holstered her gun and held open her arms, her smile growing into a wide grin. "Oh, by Qalani's eyelashes, *is it good to see yoooooooou!*"

Aly and I flew into her embrace and hugged her tight. Torquin shifted from side to side in an elephant-like way and cocked his head curiously, which was about as close as he got to cuddly. It took Nirvana a moment to recognize him. "Whoa, is that Torkissimo? What happened, dude—someone stick your face in a jet engine?"

"Um . . ."

As the big guy formulated an answer, Aly shook her head sadly, looking at our friend's gaunt figure. "I could feel the bones through your shirt, Nirvana."

"So we gave up fine dining for the cause," Nirvana said with a laugh. "Girl, I can't believe this! How on earth did you guys get here? How did you take out those Massa? *Oh who cares, I am so happy to see you!*" She turned and called over her shoulder, *"Guys! It's Aly and Jack! And a radically reimagined Torquin!"*

A chorus of screams echoed through the woods again, but this time it wasn't monkeys. I saw Fritz the mechanic, Hiro the martial arts guy, Brutus the chef, and an architect I'd once met whose name was Lisa. Their smiles beamed through sunken, grime-covered faces. They mobbed us, high-fiving and whooping at the top of their lungs.

Behind them were Eloise and Cass. "Where were you?" I called out.

"They ambushed us, thinking we were Massa," Cass said. "Eloise screamed."

"You screamed!" Eloise said.

But Cass had recognized Nirvana and was running into her arms, shrieking with joy.

"Pile up!" boomed Marco.

As he jumped into the group, nearly knocking us all over, Nirvana shot Cass and me a nervous glance.

"Marco's one of us again," Cass explained.

"Are you sure?" she asked.

I shrugged. "Can we be sure of anything?"

"Word." Nirvana, Cass, and I silently looked at the small, ragged group. Everyone seemed so happy. But the ripped clothing and haggard bodies made it clear that the rebels had been through some tough times.

One of them, I noticed, was missing. "Where's Fiddle?" I asked.

Nirvana's eyes darted back in the direction they'd come. "Come on. He'll want to see you."

As she pulled me through the rejoicing crowd, I called out for Aly, Cass, and Marco. Together we ran to the fire, which was in a small clearing. One of the Karai medical staff was hunched over Fiddle's body—someone I vaguely remembered seeing at the hospital back in the Karai days. "How's he doing, Bones?" Nirvana asked.

"The fever spiked again," the doctor replied, her face drawn and hollow. "One hundred four and rising."

Nirvana squeezed her eyes shut. "He insisted on coming with us. I knew he was too sick. I shouldn't have let him."

By now my two friends were kneeling by our side.

Three friends. I had to include Marco now.

"What happened to him?" Aly asked.

Bones sighed. "It's the jungle. There are disease-carrying insects, birds, mammals, poisonous berries. It could be any of those things. I wish I could diagnose him properly, but we're nowhere near any equipment or medical supplies. He's been like this for a while. Coming out with us was not a good idea."

"Will he be okay?" Aly said, smoothing out Fiddle's hair across his forehead. "Hey, buddy, can you hear me? What can we do for you?"

"I could use"—Fiddle struggled for words, his eyes blinking—"a burrito."

Aly smiled. "We're out of chicken. Will monkey meat be okay?"

Fiddle's glance moved from her to Marco to Cass to me. "Okay, tacos . . . instead."

"It's us, Fiddle!" I said. "Jack, Aly, Cass, Marco, and Torquin."

His eyes seemed to flash with recognition. "Can't . . . believe this . . ." he rasped. "The fearsome fivesome . . ."

He laughed, but the laugh made him cough. The cough quickly grew until his body was spasming and his soot-darkened face began turning red. Nirvana quickly reached into a weather-beaten sack, pulled out some kind of animal bladder, and began squeezing water into his mouth. "You're going to make it," she said.

263

He moved his mouth as if to respond, but he gagged. His head jerked upward and his arms and legs twitched. I could see Dr. Bones racing over as his body went limp and his eyes rolled back into his head.

"Fiddle? *Fiddle, do you hear me?*" Dr. Bones slapped his face, then grabbed his wrist briefly to feel for a pulse. Almost immediately she let go and leaned hard into his chest, pumping it three times, and then three times again.

"Yo, let's bring him to the waterfall!" Marco blurted out, reaching for Fiddle's shoulders. "That thing put me back together again."

"No, Marco, it won't work for him—you're a *Select*," Aly said. "It works for us, not for normal people."

"Cass," I said. "The shard!"

Cass swallowed. "I don't know, Jack . . ."

"Just give it to me!"

Cass reached into his pocket and pulled out a small plastic pouch that contained the fused, pebble-sized shard. I spilled it into my palm and ran around to the opposite side of Fiddle's body from Dr. Bones. Falling to my knees, I pressed the shard to his abdomen. I could feel the little remnant begin to shrink again. "Come on . . ." I murmured. "Come on, Fiddle . . ."

"Works for Select only," Torquin said, "like waterfall?"

Aly shook her head. "No, Loculi are different. The touch of a Select lets the power of the Loculus flow through. But

264

this one's wasting away. We need the other pieces. *Where are the other pieces? Where's the sack?*"

"I left the backpack by the swamp," I said.

"I'll get it!" Cass said.

As he ran back, I kept pressing the shard until I felt nothing. The doctor, still holding on to Fiddle's wrist, placed his arm down on the ground and shook her head.

I pulled away and sat back. Overhead the monkeys fell silent. As if they knew. Fiddle's mouth was open, his eyes staring upward and his brow beetled as if he'd noticed the silence, too.

Something the size of a seat cushion landed softly on my shoulder, and I knew it was Torquin's hand. "Good try, Jack," he said softly.

All around me, heads bowed and tears ran runnels through dirt-stained faces.

I opened my palm. At the center was a small, colorless dot, about the size of a sesame seed.

CHAPTER FORTY

THE LABYRINTH AND THE TAPESTRY

"HERE IT IS!" Cass shouted, running toward me with the sack containing the shards. When he saw Fiddle, he stopped short. "Is he . . . ?"

"I'm sorry . . ." I murmured, both to Fiddle and to my friends. "I'm so sorry."

Eloise burst into tears. "I never saw a dead person before . . ."

Cass put an awkward arm around her shoulder. As the KI people gathered around the body, one of them held some kind of makeshift torch. Fiddle's features seemed to flutter in the light of the flame.

"My best friend on the whole island . . ." Nirvana said, swallowing a sob. "I was such a brat when I got here. He schooled me."

"I don't know why the shard didn't work," I said. "It worked with Aly . . ."

"Maybe too small," Torquin suggested.

I stared at the tiny, freckle-sized dot in my palm. "I could have run for the other shards sooner. What was I thinking? I killed him . . ."

"The shards are locked in a box, Jack," Cass said. "It's not your fault he died."

"If it's anyone's fault, it's mine," Marco said. "I never should have left you guys in the first place."

"Stop it," Aly said. "It's done. We can't just stay here. How long till Dimitrios wakes up, or till the Massa back at camp come after the missing goons—"

"Or come after the missing Loculi," Cass added.

Nirvana stood. "We'll take Fiddle into the headquarters and bury him there. Let's move."

Marco crouched down and lifted up Fiddle's shoulders. "Help me lift him, Tork."

"I'll grab some flashlights from the Massa," I said.

Fritz nodded grimly. "I'll get their weapons."

* * *

Grieving would have to wait. Speed and silence were crucial.

We hit the path with only a few flashlights as guides, to conserve batteries. Mine was already almost dead. The walk was silent and steady. Marco held Fiddle's arms and Torquin his legs. Aly and I stayed together, while behind us Cass and Eloise walked single file among the other Karai.

I could not shake the image of Fiddle's body going slack.

"Penny for your thoughts," Aly said.

I smiled and shook my head, concentrating on the narrow path.

"Okay, a dollar." I felt her slipping her fingers into mine. "Hey. Mr. Moody Broody. It's not your fault."

"Right." I took a deep breath. "We . . . we have to look on the bright side."

"Yes," Aly said.

"We found the rebels," I said.

"And got Marco back again," Aly added.

I nodded. "Also, my mom turned out not to be evil after all."

"Exactly!" Aly said. "Plus we have the two Loculi back, *and* all the shards."

"And I guess I'll be king soon," I added, forcing a smile.

"Heaven help us all," Aly muttered.

We were at the base of Mount Onyx now. The volcano's peak rose pitch-black against the star-freckled sky. Nirvana's flashlight beam strafed the vines and bushes lining the sides. When the vegetation gave way to an expanse of silver-gray rock, we stopped. Above us, a deep crevice in the rock formed a giant seven. The bottom of the seven's diagonal pointed to a small bush that seemed to have grown into the wall, about eye level.

I knew immediately that the bush must have been fake. Under it was a carving of a griffin's head, which was actually a secret keyhole into the volcano's inner labyrinth.

Aly looked around nervously. "No cameras?"

Nirvana eyed the trees. "One," she said. "But we moved it."

She reached into her shoulder bag and pulled out a familiar-looking rock that contained a code left by Herman Wenders, the discoverer of the island. "Can I do the honors?" I said.

"Quickly," Nirvana said, shoving the black stone into my hand.

I inserted the stone into the carving. With a deep scraping noise, the entrance slowly slid open.

As the black triangle opened into the thick inner wall of the mountain, a gust of cool, vaguely rotten-smelling air blasted out. Nirvana looked nervously over her shoulder. "It's a miracle the Massa haven't found this yet."

She went in first, followed by Marco and Torquin with Fiddle's body, then the other Karai rebels.

Cass, Aly, and I hung for a moment at the dark entrance. "I hate this place," Cass said, gazing in at the dark, mossy-walled corridor of the labyrinth. "I almost died in here."

Aly nodded. "Marco *did* die."

The memories flooded out like ghosts in the rock: Cass on fire, screaming with pain. Marco's body, limp and crushed after a fall into the volcano. The waterfall that miraculously healed them both. Back then the journey was baffling, with the promise of death at every wrong turn.

But now, as we finally entered, we were following a group who had walked the path a hundred times. "Welcome back," I said.

The air quickly grew stale in the narrow passage. I avoided stepping into the crevice where Aly had long ago dropped her flashlight. I caught the acrid smell of roasted bat guano, from the wrong turn that had led to Cass's accident. In one of the other intersecting paths, I saw the skeleton of a horse-sized animal. Yet another contained a set of manacles bolted into the wall. "Ch-ch-cheery, huh?" Cass said.

I kept a quick pace, but I had to slow down at the entrance to one of the side tunnels. Just inside it hung a large, faded, ancient tapestry. We'd seen a work like this before, but it had burned in the guano fire. This one was different. It depicted a fierce argument between the king and queen. Qalani was standing regally behind the Heptakiklos, which was filled with seven glowing Loculi of different, rich colors. Beside her was Massarym, kneeling before the creation, with an expression of awe. In the foreground, King Uhla'ar pointed at them with furious accusation. His face was stern and sharp boned, his eyebrows arched and his hair thickly curled.

There was something familiar about the face, but I couldn't put my finger on it.

"Jack! What are you doing?" Aly cried out.

"I'm looking . . ." I said, tilting my head toward the tapestry. "Why do I think I've seen this guy before?"

"Because, duh, it's Uhla'ar, and you've been dreaming about him since Bodrum," she said, grabbing my arm. "Now come on. We'll do the museum tour later."

She pulled me away, but the face was stuck in my head. The dream had been vivid; Aly was right about that. But I wasn't sure that was it. I felt like I'd met this guy.

We caught up with the others and trudged over cold stone toward the center. I'd forgotten how long the path was. Even with people who knew the way, it seemed to take forever.

I knew we were close to the center when I felt a prickling sensation in my brain that grew to a steady hum.

Aly gave me a look. "You've got that Song-of-the-Heptakiklos expression on your face. Either that or diarrhea."

"Don't you hear it, too?" I asked.

Aly shrugged. "Cass, Marco, and I—not being king material—we have to be right on top of it to hear it. You go ahead of me."

I walked forward. The sound seeped into me, like little

gremlins twanging the nerves of my brain.

Soon the Song was mixed with the whoosh of falling water. Just ahead, Marco and Torquin had stopped by the edge of the waterfall's pool. Marco was holding Fiddle's wrists with one hand now, and with the other he stooped to splash water onto Fiddle's face. "I know, I know, you said it won't work," he said. "But I had to try."

"Okay," Torquin said quietly, "but we go."

He and Marco continued onward with Fiddle's body, into the caldera.

I had to adjust to the eerie glow. It was the dead of night, but the moon seemed to be concentrating its rays here, making the whole place glow green-gold as if the walls themselves held light.

"Did you ever try to imagine what this must have been like?" Cass whispered. "I mean, back when it was the center of a whole continent?"

"It was a valley . . ." I said. "Beautiful, too, with tall trees ringing the top, and a carpet of flowers . . ."

My early dreams of Atlantis were so vivid I felt like I'd been there. I would always be running through that valley toward my own death. Talking about it scared me.

But I had no fear right now. I had work to do.

Marco and Torquin settled Fiddle down by the vast, rounded wall. Lisa and Fritz began digging a grave, using a shovel and a pickax.

Nirvana looked away, her lip quivering. "Well," she said, trying to be cheerful, "shall we show you around our vast complex?"

She and Hiro began lighting torches that were made of dried thatch set on tripods of tree branches. A motley collection of tools had been propped up against the caldera walls, along with a few pots and some canvas bags.

"These contain dried food—hardtack, pemmican," Nirvana explained. "The stuff is pretty foul but edible. Way back when, Professor Bhegad and the old-timers made sure to hide emergency supplies in some undisclosed locations. Fiddle was the only one who knew how to get to those places. We have some communications, but it's all pretty basic."

I followed her to a table made of three flat rocks. On it was an old laptop connected to a set of wires, a heavy-duty battery, and an antenna made of wire hangers and tinfoil. Next to the table were three other spare batteries. "Needless to say, no internet," Nirvana went on. "But we use walkie-talkies to keep in touch on recon operations. Two of our best people, Bird Eye and Squawker, are out in the field now. They're keeping an eye on Dimitrios and the sleeping beauties. If anything bad happens, we'll know. Unfortunately, we have to be careful about energy—everything's shut off most of the time, except for extreme emergencies."

"Wow . . ." Aly said. "Stone Age living."

Nirvana laughed. "That's me, Wilma Flintstone."

As they went back to talking tech, I walked toward the shadows at the rear of the caldera. The Song was deafening, drawing me to its source. A strange mist rose from the shadows, disappearing upward in swirling wisps. I hadn't seen the Heptakiklos since our last visit, and I had no real reason to see it now. But I couldn't help wanting to.

As I got closer, the mist cleared. I saw the outline of the round temple, sunken into the rock floor. It seemed to glow from a light source below the surface of the earth.

It was the place where Queen Qalani had first harnessed the energy of Atlantis into the seven Loculi. And it had sat empty ever since Massarym had stolen them away.

I knew not to touch the shaft. I'd pulled the whole thing out once before. It had opened the rift and allowed the griffin to fly through. Professor Bhegad called this a space-time flux point—yet another wonderful horrible thing that only Select could access.

This time we had two Loculi. Three, if we could put together the Loculus of Healing. Once we got the boxes open and reconstructed the Loculus of Healing—*if* that was still possible—we could insert them in their places. I was dying to do that ASAP.

Three Loculi was three-sevenths of the way to completion. Or .428571. Forty-three percent.

Almost half.

"Jack?" Marco's voice called out. "You let a griffin loose and I will personally pound your head into oatmeal."

I began to back away. From behind me came the sharp chink . . . chink . . . chink . . . of the digging. Marco was waiting nervously. "Let's see if we can put together Number Three," I called out.

Aly crouched by the wall, opening the canvas bag to reveal the three boxes. Each was sealed by a thick brass latch with a metal LCD plate. Under each plate was a number keypad. "What the—?"

"I know the codes." Nirvana ran over. She began tapping out numbers on the pad, and finally let out a big groan. "Great. First they steal these lockboxes from us, and then go and reprogram the locks! That's military-grade encryption. We'll never get it."

Aly nodded thoughtfully. "Give me a few minutes."

She pulled back a chair and sat at the table, jiggling the laptop's mouse. Numbers began flowing down the screen like a weird digital rainstorm.

"That'll take days," Nirvana said, "even with our encryption software."

"Not if I improve the software," Aly said, her fingers clattering on the keyboard.

"I have a better idea." Marco shoved the boxes back into the sack, strapped it to his belt, and began climbing the caldera wall. "Bet you I can get to the top and drop these babies before you finish. That'll open them."

"Whoa, Marco, no!" I shouted.

Cass and I ran to the wall. But Marco was quicker by far. He dug his hands and feet into the crevices and jutting roots, as if he were climbing a ladder.

Aly looked up from the desk. My heart was quickening, and I had a realization—something I hadn't wanted to admit till now. "I'm still not sure I trust him," I whispered. "What if he escapes?"

I expected them to argue. Aly had a crush on Marco,

that much I knew. Cass idolized him. But neither of them disagreed. There wasn't much we could do. None of us could possibly follow him.

As we all watched him, I tried to mentally block the Song of the Heptakiklos, which was giving me a headache. But now another sound was almost drowning it out—a distant, steady rumbling from above.

"What the heck is that?" Cass murmured.

"A plane?" Nirvana said.

Nirvana's walkie-talkie squawked, and she picked it up. "Base."

A tinny reply echoed through the caldera. "Bird Eye. Unknown craft in island airspace. Repeat . . . aircraft overhead!"

Nirvana frowned. "Copy. Is the craft Massa, Bird Eye?"

"Negative," the voice crackled in response. "It looks . . . military? Maybe trying for a beach landing?"

"Military?" Nirvana said.

"Greek."

"That's impossible."

A tremendous boom shook the mountain, nearly knocking me off my feet. Above us, Marco screamed in surprise. Rocks and soil tumbled down the side of the caldera, landing in clouds of dust.

Nirvana dropped the walkie-talkie. *"I don't think it's a beach landing!"* she cried out. *"It just crashed!"*

CHAPTER FORTY-ONE

IS NOT GORILLA

"MARCO!" ALY SCREAMED up into the caldera.

Nirvana shone her flashlight upward, pinning Marco in its beam. The crash had shaken him away from the wall. He swayed back and forth in the air, gripping a tree root. The bag of Loculi came crashing down, landing on the ground with a sharp clatter. *"They couldn't use the airport?"* he called down.

"Marco, get down now!" I said.

"Yeah, I was thinking the same thing!" Marco managed to grab a sturdier root with his free hand, then dig his feet into the wall. In a few seconds, he was heading steadily downward.

Aly turned back to her screen. "Okay, good news, guys.

The Massa have a limited-range VPN, which means probably some sort of satellite rig accessing a small part of the broadband spectrum. If I use command-line code to avoid the GUI, I think I can exploit security holes in the back end and avoid detection, at least temporarily."

Cass and I looked over her shoulder. "And the English translation?" Cass said.

"I'm able to hack into their system," Aly said, typing lines of code into a black screen, "including the surveillance network. I'm trying to locate the video feeds from those cameras they planted in the jungle. Maybe one of them will let us see our location. And we'll identify what just happened. The problem is, everything's labeled randomly. Hang on, I'll scroll through them . . ."

The lines of code vanished, and eight small images appeared. All of them were practically pitch-black—except for the scene in the lower left, which showed a flash of bright orange.

Aly clicked on it. The image filled the screen, showing the black cone of Mount Onyx against the gray sky—and a plume of smoke rising from flames near the top of the volcano.

She zoomed in. Flaming chunks of airplane wreckage dotted the bushes. Above them, the outline of a small tail section emerged from a cluster of trees, ringed by flame. It looked exactly like the planes I'd seen overhead while we were outside Routhouni.

I was staring so closely at the wreck, I almost didn't notice a small gray shadow moving through the nearby trees.

"Is that a person?" I asked.

"Unless a gorilla flew the plane," Aly said.

"Possible, considering the landing technique," Cass said.

Now the whole group was gathered around Aly, including the gravediggers—and Marco, covered with dirt.

"Pay attention." Aly zoomed as close as she could on the small, moving blotch. But it wasn't going downward. "It's *climbing*."

"Is not gorilla," Torquin grumbled.

"Is there a camera at the top of the volcano?" Cass asked.

Nirvana shook her head. "There were three. But we destroyed them."

"How about on the sides?" Aly began typing in more commands. "Okay. I'm picking up feeds from a couple of locations on the volcano slope . . . hang on . . ."

As Aly clicked, three completely black images showed on her laptop screen. She was about to click away from them when I thought I saw a small movement in the middle one. "Hold it. On that one. Can you adjust the brightness?"

Aly clicked on the middle image. It filled the screen. With a few more clicks, she managed to make the blackness a lot lighter, but it was extremely grainy. "This is the best I can do. The moonlight helps."

I leaned closer. A silvery figure was making its way

slowly up the side of the mountain. Definitely human. And quickly passing upward and out of the frame.

"Let me access the camera's remote motion control," Aly said. "I think I can swivel it."

The image vibrated as the camera began to turn. For a long moment everything was a blur, until the lens pointed directly up the slope.

The tree cover was sparse, the flat summit of Mount Onyx visible at the top. The moon must have been directly over the frame, because the figure was using the light to climb. There was no doubt now that it was a man.

We watched silently as he hauled himself over the rim of Mount Onyx, where he stood to full height. A leather sack, cinched with rope, was slung over his shoulders. Silhouetted by the moon, he turned in the direction of the camera, and I got a good view of a few characteristics.

Thick beard. Bare calves. Sandals.

"I don't believe this . . ." I murmured under my breath.

As the man glanced over the island below, he threw back his head and opened his mouth wide. From above us, we heard a muffled cry that echoed a fraction of a second later through the video feed:

"ATLAAANNNNTIS!"

"If I'm dreaming, someone kick me awake," Aly said. "And if not—ladies and gentlemen, meet Zeus."

"Zeus?" Nirvana said.

"How did he get here?" Cass asked.

"Wait," Marco said. "Did you say *Zeus*? Like the god of all awesomeness who never really existed but they made a statue of him at Olympia which became one of the Seven Wonders? *That* Zeus?"

"While you were babysitting rug rats, we found that statue, Marco," Aly said. "It has the fourth Loculus. Which I'm willing to bet is in his sack."

"Who are you calling a rug rat?" Eloise shouted.

"But . . . it's a statue!" Marco said. "Since when do statues fly planes?"

"Since when do statues rise out of rock piles, and ancient civilizations hang out across rivers, and zombies frolic underground?" Cass asked. "Since when do normal kids develop superpowers?"

"Good point," Marco said.

We looked closely at the bushy beard, the angular face with its straight nose and close-cropped hair. No question that it was the creature that had chased us in Routhouni.

But he was reminding me of someone else, too.

"The face in the tapestry . . ." I said.

"The who?" Marco asked.

"Back in the labyrinth," I said. "There was a portrait. It was the same face."

"A portrait of Zeus," Aly drawled. "How original."

"You don't understand," I replied. "This guy is not Zeus."

Aly and Nirvana peeled their eyes from the screen. They, Cass, Marco, and Eloise looked at me as if I'd grown antlers. "Um, Jack, if you recall, the statue moved from Olympia," Aly said. "We saw proof. It had a Loculus."

"My dream . . ." I said. "It's all making sense now. I was Massarym. The king had put a curse on me and I cursed him back."

Nirvana looked at Aly, jacking a thumb in my direction. "Has he gotten this weird just recently?"

"The statue was a big hunk of marble," I went on. "And somehow I—I mean, Massarym—was able to cast him inside it."

"Jack, what does that have to do with this?" Aly said.

I put my hand on the screen, where the man was walking to the edge of the caldera, looking down.

Looking toward us.

"Massarym imprisoned his own father in stone—turned him into a statue," I said. "That statue isn't Zeus. It's the king of Atlantis."

CHAPTER FORTY-TWO

THE TEFLON KING

"BROTHER JACK, HAVE you been inhaling too much Heptakiklos gas?" Marco asked. "I mean, the statue was official. The Statue of Zeus. So if it wasn't really him, wouldn't people see the face and wonder, hey, why is this other guy's face on the statue?"

Aly dropped her head into her hands. "Zeus is mythological, Marco! No one knew what he looked like!"

"In Greece, no one knew what King Uhla'ar looked like either," I pointed out. "So Massarym could call the statue whatever he wanted."

No one said a word. On the screen, Uhla'ar was disappearing from the frame. Downward.

We looked up. Way at the top of the caldera, barely

visible in the moonlight, a tiny black shadow made its way toward us.

"By the blood of Karai, what does he want from us?" Nirvana added.

"How did he get hold of a plane—and fly it?" Eloise asked.

"How could he be alive at all?" Aly asked.

"So . . . is actually *Uhla'ar* statue, not Zeus statue?" Torquin said.

"Personally, I am finding this hard to follow," Marco said.

"I don't know why he's here!" I said. "All I know is that we found the statue in some cheesy village in Greece, where he spent the last few decades watching TV."

Marco spun toward me. "Okay, so the way I'm seeing it, this is great, right? You said this thing had a fourth Loculus. That's . . . ewoksapoppin'! Wait. What's the word, Cass?"

"Emosewa," Cass piped up.

"Emosewa," Marco said. "The guy is handing it to us!"

A small shower of rocks and soil fell from above, crashing to the ground in a small cloud. Nirvana shone her flashlight upward. The light barely reached the top, just enough to silhouette the king as his sandaled feet dug into the sides of the caldera.

"Yo!" Marco called up. "'Sup, King Ooh!"

"He doesn't understand!" Aly said.

"Sorry," Marco replied. "Lo! Greetings, yonder king! What a big Loculus thou hast. Canst we holdeth it?"

In response, Uhla'ar plucked a rock from the soil and flung it downward.

"King does not come in peace," Torquin said.

"By the way, Marco, there's one problem," Cass said. "It's the Loculus of Strength. Just in case you're planning to tie him up like a vromaski."

Eloise was trembling. "Maybe I could try biting him?"

The king descended slowly, the Loculus sack bouncing on his back, and I had an idea. "I don't know why he's here, but something tells me he's not going to give up that Loculus. Marco, if we get him to drop it, could you catch it?"

Marco smiled. "If it's not falling fast enough to burn in the atmosphere, yeah, it's mine."

My eyes darted toward a pile of Karai equipment against the wall, stuff the rebels had managed to salvage. I ran over, quickly rummaging through coils of wire, sections of rubber hose, tools, and metal frames.

There.

I pulled out a small Y-shaped pipe riddled with holes along each side. It looked like part of an old sprinkler. I never thought that in a tropical rain forest the Karai would have to use sprinklers.

Grabbing a length of rubber hose, I quickly tied one end to each section of the Y.

Perfect slingshot.

"David?" I said, handing it to Marco along with a baseball-sized rock.

Marco looked at it blankly for a second, then smiled. "Ohhhhh, I got it . . ." Nestling the rock into the hose, he held the contraption upward, pointing it at Uhla'ar. Then he pulled the hose back . . . back . . . "Right upside Goliath's head, Brother," he said.

As he let go, the rock hurtled into the darkness.

I could hear the dull *thwock* on the back of Uhla'ar's head. The old man let out a cry of surprise, then turned his face toward us and shouted in obvious anger. I couldn't hear what he was saying, but in Nirvana's flashlight beam I could see him swinging the sack around. He was cradling the Loculus like a football, as if he were trying to protect it. I could now see that the sack had been cut in several places, like preslashed jeans. Which meant his fingers were in contact with the object inside.

"What do you guys think you're doing?" Aly said, racing toward us. "You want to kill him?"

"The guy's Teflon," Marco said. "He survived a bazillion years."

"You're just getting him angrier!" Aly said. "What if he's here to help? What if he wants to return the Loculus to the Heptakiklos?"

Using his free hand, Uhla'ar was moving like a spider,

clutching tree roots with his fingers, leaping from one foot-hold to the other with perfect precision. Like a dancer on steroids.

Marco dropped the slingshot. "Holy mutation. He's climbing down with one hand. Who does he think he is—*me?*"

We all backed off. In a few moments, King Uhla'ar landed on the caldera floor with a solid thud. He faced Marco, his eyes red and accusing.

"'Sup, Spidey?" Marco said.

As he walked forward, his hands still tucked into the slashes of the sack, Uhla'ar glared at us silently. "What's with his eyes?" Marco said. "They're all swirly."

"He's not human!" Aly said.

"Does he understand English?" Marco asked.

"He's been watching lots of TV," I replied.

"Okay, that makes total sense," Marco said.

Aly stepped forward toward Uhla'ar. "Greetings, O Great King of Atlantis, trapped cruelly in stone and now released just in time to restore the Loculi to their rightful places. We greet thee with joyful open arms."

"Get to the point," Cass hissed.

Holding the sack tightly, the king turned slowly to Aly. His eyes were like small torches. He didn't react to her words, but instead began walking directly toward her, as if she weren't there.

She jumped away. Uhla'ar was heading straight for the center of the caldera.

For the Heptakiklos.

In my ears, the Song was like a scream now. I could see Uhla'ar shaking his head, hesitating. He must have been hearing it, too. Aly's face was creased with worry, but Cass put an arm around her. "He's putting it back," Cass said.

"I thought he was supposed to hold and protect it," Aly replied. "He killed that guy centuries ago who tried to take it. He tried to kill us."

I thought about the dream. About how the king blamed Massarym for the island's destruction. Uhla'ar wanted one thing only—to undo what his son had done. To return the Loculi to Atlantis.

"He's no dumb statue, Aly," I said. "He's Uhla'ar. He was protecting the Loculus for himself—so that one day he could bring it back to his homeland."

"Jack, this is amazing," Aly said. "He's helping us. We've been going after all these Wonders to fight for the Loculi. Now one of the Wonders is bringing a Loculus to us!"

Aly, Cass, Marco, Nirvana, and I followed Uhla'ar. Could it be? Not long ago we were as good as dead. Now we had a chance of being more than halfway to our goal.

Four Loculi.

My heart was pounding so hard, I wasn't even thinking about the Song. Uhla'ar stopped at the edge of the

Heptakiklos. The rift light surrounded him in an amber-green halo, flickering in the mist.

He set the bag down and bent over the Heptakiklos. Then, wrapping his fingers around the broken blade, he began to pull.

Marco was the first to run forward. He grabbed the king's shoulder. "Whoa, that's a nasty mistake. Trust us."

The king whirled on Marco. With his free hand, he grabbed Marco by the collar and lifted him clear off the ground. *"MAKE MY DAY."*

CHAPTER FORTY-THREE

BRAGGART, TRAITOR, DESERTER, KILLER?

TORQUIN RAN FORWARD to help, but Marco managed to shake himself loose from the king's grip. "Stay back, Red Beard! I can handle this guy."

"We need backup!" Nirvana cried out to the other rebels.

As Uhla'ar turned back to the rift, Marco grabbed him in a headlock. The king roared, but Marco held tight, pulling him back . . .

Back . . .

They were clear of the mist now, clear of the light. With a powerful thrust, Marco threw the king away from the Heptakiklos, toward the middle of the caldera. *Just stay away!* Marco yelled. *What is wrong with you?*

The king landed hard and rolled, then sprang to his feet.

Nirvana was holding a crankshaft now, Fritz a rusted metal pipe. The rebels were all armed with the detritus of the old headquarters.

"What are you doing?" I said.

"We need that Loculus," Nirvana replied. "We've worked hard. Our ancestors have worked hard. We don't need him to ruin everything for us."

"He's the king!" I replied.

"Not anymore," she said.

Uhla'ar's eyes scanned across the line of Karai. Marco stood solidly between the king and the Heptakiklos. *"AT . . . LANTIS . . ."* the king growled, unsheathing the dagger from his belt.

Its hilt was huge, weirdly large for a knife that size. It housed a jagged blade, twisted and sharp like a broken bottle.

"What the—?" Marco sputtered.

"Watch out!" Aly shouted.

Marco darted over toward the Karai pile and pulled out a long, hooked crowbar. Leaping between the Karai and the king, he thrust it toward Uhla'ar's head like a sword.

The king's free arm seemed to vanish for a moment as it moved to block the attack. With a sharp clank, the dagger stopped the thrust and sent Marco sprawling.

"COWABUNNNNGAAAAA!" King Uhla'ar said, charging toward Marco again.

Marco spun around, took two steps toward the wall, then leaped. His head snapped backward as he took three gravity-defying steps up the wall. With a powerful thrust, he backflipped over the head of Uhla'ar.

The king's jagged blade jammed into the dirt wall.

"Enough!" Torquin grumbled. As Marco landed, the big guy lunged for the king. He wrapped his thick arms around Uhla'ar and threw him to the ground. The king landed with a loud thud, inches from the sack he had carried here on his shoulders.

The Loculus.

I dived for it at the same time Marco did. He managed to grab the fabric first, pulling the Loculus out of the sack.

"*ARRRGGGHHH!*" The king's cry echoed in the caldera as he sprang to his feet, pulled his stuck dagger from the wall, and started for Marco.

Marco tucked the Loculus of Strength under his left arm. Wheeling around, he twisted away from Uhla'ar's thrust. The blade flashed. Blood sprayed from Marco's leg. Now Torquin was coming at the king again, holding aloft a long mallet with a thick metal head.

Uhla'ar turned calmly to face the big man. As Torquin's powerful blow flashed downward, the king ducked. With a swift, continuous move, he grabbed Torquin's arm and threw him against the wall. His head hit the stone with a dull thud, and he fell limply to the ground.

No.

I picked up a rock, reared back with my arm, and threw it at Uhla'ar. It connected with his shoulder, and he stumbled.

"Steee-rike, Brother Jack!" Marco said. Holding the crowbar aloft with his right hand, his leg red with blood, he lunged at the king and swung hard. With a loud clank, Marco knocked the dagger out of the king's hand.

Uhla'ar was weaponless now. His eyes were fixed in the direction of the Heptakiklos. "He's not going to cooperate," Marco said, clutching and unclutching the crowbar. "He's *obsessed* with that thing . . ."

"Please, Marco, you're losing a lot of blood!" Dr. Bones called out.

Marco blinked hard, as if trying to maintain his balance. A pool of blood gathered below his foot. "I've got the Loculus of Strength, baby, I'm good."

As the king leaped toward the Heptakiklos again, Marco blocked him. Both thumped to the ground. The crowbar went flying, but Marco held tight to the Loculus. With his right hand now free, he pinned the king by the neck to the ground. "Sorry, dude," he said. "If you're not going to cooperate, we have to take you out."

"Marco, you're choking him!" Aly yelled. *"Have you gone crazy? He was the king of Atlantis!"*

I raced toward him. As Marco pressed harder on the

294

neck, Uhla'ar's legs kicked like beached fish. The king began to raise his arm as if to strike out, but instead it fell to the side.

I wrapped my fingers around the Loculus. Marco wouldn't let go, but the orb's power jolted through me, too. I yanked him upward by the collar and he flew backward, tumbling toward the shadows.

"Jack . . . ?" he said in disbelief.

The king's body was slack. His chest was still.

Marco groaned, clutching his injured leg. Dr. Bones raced to his side, quickly wrapping the injury with a tourniquet.

Cass stared at the king. "Is he . . . ?"

Racing over to Uhla'ar, the doctor placed her fingers against his neck. "No pulse."

"I—I didn't know he could die . . ." Aly said.

I set the Loculus down against the wall, not far from Marco. We had it in our possession now, and that was good. But I didn't feel any sense of triumph. "He was *there*, when it happened to Atlantis," I said. "He could have told us so much. Answered so many questions."

"Professor Bhegad . . . Fiddle . . . now the king of Atlantis," Aly said. "All dead. When does it stop?"

Eloise was whimpering, standing with her fists clutched to her sides. "My second dead person ever."

All of our eyes were locked on Marco. Slumped against

the wall, he seemed to fold into himself. I wasn't sure who I was looking at anymore. He'd been a protector and friend. He'd been a braggart, a traitor, and a deserter.

But he'd never been a killer.

"I—I had to do it . . ." Marco stood slowly, backing away from the body along the wall. As he glanced at us, from face to face, we turned away. No one knew what to say.

I kept my glance focused on the body of the king. In death, the anger was gone from his face. He looked handsome, wise, and weirdly familiar.

It took awhile for me to realize he actually resembled my dad.

Behind me, the grave digging had begun again. There would be two bodies now. I figured I'd have to help.

As I got up to go, I finally turned away from the fallen king.

But not before I saw his fingers twitch.

CHAPTER FORTY-FOUR

THE SWORD AND THE RIFT

"HE'S FAKING!"

My shout rang through the caldera.

But it was too late. King Uhla'ar was on his feet, with a clear path to the Heptakiklos.

"No-o-o-o!" Aly was the closest. Screaming, she ran to block his way.

We all converged toward him. But Uhla'ar grabbed her by the neck, holding his dagger high. *"I . . . will . . . kill . . ."* he said.

My feet dug into the ground. All of us stopped. "Let her go," I said.

The king didn't reply. Instead, he dragged Aly with him, toward the rift. She was trying to say something, but

Uhla'ar had her tight around the neck. Her face was reddening by the second.

Out of the corner of my eye, I could see Fritz the mechanic lifting a gun. "Don't do it!" I called out. "It won't affect him, and you might hit Aly."

"We have to do something," Nirvana said.

I stepped toward Uhla'ar, reaching toward Aly. "Give her back to us, Uhla'ar. Release her and go ahead. Open the rift."

Uhla'ar smiled.

"Jack, no!" Nirvana cried out.

With a rough shove, the king threw Aly toward me. As she stumbled into my arms, he leaped toward the rift, his snaggletoothed dagger in hand. From the center rift, the mist rose like coiled fingers. The piece in the middle, the broken blade I'd idiotically pulled out when I first got here, was glowing brightly.

Slowly the king turned, pointing his broken dagger toward the blade at the center of the Heptakiklos. Two arched lines of white, like evil smiles, leaped upward from the edge of the blade. I could see now that the jagged edge of his dagger had not been designed that way. It matched exactly the pattern of the blade in the ground.

It wasn't a dagger at all. It was the missing half of a sword that had long ago been split in two.

A flare of bright white engulfed the space between the

blades. Uhla'ar lurched forward, nearly losing his balance. He cried out with pain but held tight to the hilt. The whiteness dissipated around him like an exploding snowball, and he stood in a blue glow.

The broken blade had pulled the dagger toward it. Now the two were fused into one long, sleek sword still stuck in the rift.

"*ISCHIS* . . ." Uhla'ar said.

Through the rift, the Song of the Heptakiklos poured out, transforming into a noise of screams and chitters and flapping wings.

I stepped toward him. "No!" I yelled. "*Whatever you do, don't pull that out!*"

Uhla'ar gave the sword a powerful yank. With a *sssshhh-iiiiick* that echoed sharply, it came out clean.

KEEEAAAHHHH!

I knew the griffin's call. I'd hoped never to hear it again. I could smell its fetid, garbage-dump odor as it swept overhead on a gust of hot wind. As I covered my head with my arms, I heard the panicked snuffling of a hose-beaked vromaski, speeding past me for the safety of the labyrinth path.

The ground shook, knocking me off my feet. A snake with the head of a fanged rat slithered past, and a winged spider with talons climbed onto my head and launched itself upward.

"*Eeeewww! Ew! Ew! Ew!*" Eloise cried.

Though the chaos of mist and flying beasts, I saw her flinging a dark, thin, furry creature to the ground. As it landed with a screech, it spit a glob of yellow liquid straight upward.

A vizzeet. We'd had way too much experience with those nasty things.

"Get away from that—it spits poison!" I shouted.

Cass was already pulling his sister to safety. But the vizzeet didn't care about either of them. It leaped up, turned, and joined two others that were already climbing the caldera walls.

I lay flat on my stomach as flapping wings tapped the top of my head. *Aly. Where was Aly?*

Marco and Cass were huddled together in a cloud of dust kicked up by a fallen chunk of wall. Nirvana was trying to protect Fiddle's body from the flying debris and crazed beasts. The other rebels were scattered about, seeking shelter. All alive.

Moving through the center of it all was King Uhla'ar. He swung his sword against the attack of a leathery, batlike creature with a human head. In midcackle it was split in two, its twitching halves flopping downward.

He was heading back to the rift. I fought back nausea as I moved through the slavering wild beasts. The rift was shaking now, the Song of the Heptakiklos drowned beneath an unearthly rumble. It was about to blow wide open. When that happened, the barrier between then and now, between Atlantis and modern times, would shatter. Time and space would fold in on themselves, and what would happen to the world then?

"You see what you did?" I shouted. *"Plug it back up!"*

As the king stood over the rift, something hurtled through the air toward him.

Aly.

The king stumbled. The sword went flying. *"Grab it, Jack!"* she said. *"He wants to go in! Grab the sword and plug it up after he leaves!"*

"What?" I said.

"He told me, 'There's no place like home'!" she shouted. *"He's trying to get back there, through the rift! That's what he wants!"*

As I ran toward the sword, Uhla'ar grabbed Aly's arm. She lifted her leg and stomped down on his sandaled foot. Hard. The king let out a roar.

She tried to wriggle free, but he held tight. A blast of silver-blue light surrounded them both like a flame. He was dragging her with him toward the rift. Aly's eyes were enormous, her mouth open in a scream. She was looking straight at me.

"NO-O-O-O-O!" I screamed.

An explosion knocked me backward, blinding me. As I staggered to my feet, my eyes adjusted. *"Alyyyy!"* I called out.

But she and Uhla'ar had both dropped out of sight.

301

CHAPTER FORTY-FIVE

SOMETHING MUCH WORSE

MY KNEES BUCKLED. I fell to the ground. I didn't even notice the swarm of hideous creatures. The ground shook once . . . twice, and it was hard to stay upright, even kneeling.

I crawled toward the Heptakiklos, my fingers wrapping themselves around worms and fur. The light from the rift was spewing upward, as if the sun itself were emerging. *"ALYYYY!"* I screamed again.

"Brother Jack, what are you doing?"

Marco. I could feel his hand on my shoulder, pulling me upward. "She's gone," I said.

"Dude, we have to close the rift!" he said. "Where's the sword?"

He didn't know. He had no idea what had just happened.

"Got it!"

That was Cass. Now I could see him racing by. He had the sword in his hand, a confused, rodentlike creature hanging onto the tip.

He and Marco, together, held the sword over the rift. With a sickening *crrrack*, it ripped open another eight or so inches. Maybe a foot. A greenish-black beast began to rise from below. It was something I'd never seen before, its head a glob of shifting shapes—eyes morphing into mouths morphing into gelatinous black pools.

I ran toward them. *"Don't do it!"*

"Don't do what?" Marco said.

"Close the rift!" I reached for the sword, but Marco pushed me away. He plunged the sword into the beast's pulsating crown. Its cry was a physical thing, shaking the ground beneath us. As I scrambled to my feet, the swirling mists began to gather. They were changing course, sucking back into the hole as if by a giant vacuum cleaner. The ground began to thrust upward, reversing its motion. The beast seemed to dissolve but the sword was holding fast.

With a snap, the rock closed around the blade like a fist.

"NO-O-O-O!" I cried out.

The Song was deafening again. The Heptakiklos was no longer oozing light but nearly blinding me with its brightness. Its faded, ancient edges seemed brand-new.

I grabbed the sword again, but Marco took my wrist. "What has gotten into you, Jack?" he pleaded.

"Aly's gone!" I said. "He took her with him!"

Cass and Marco both went pale. Marco let go of my hand.

I didn't care if the rift opened. I didn't care what kind of beast came through. We could not leave her.

304

As I gripped the sword, the ground juddered beneath us. My hands slipped and my legs gave way.

We all hit the floor, Torquin landing with a dusty thump. "Earthquake?" he mumbled.

I felt hands grabbing my arms. The rebels had surrounded me. Nirvana's face was bone white. "Jack, you can't open that rift again," she said. "This is not an earthquake."

"Then what is it?" Marco said.

A pine tree, dislodged from the top of the volcano, came crashing down behind us.

"It's something much worse!" Nirvana said. "Out of here—now—before the whole thing collapses!"

Epilogue

WHEN WE GOT to the shore, Mom was there. She stood shoulder to shoulder with Number One. Brother Dimitrios sat by the edge of the jungle along with his cronies, attended to by Massa health workers.

When Mom saw me, she came running. "We lost Aly . . ." I said.

I think she already knew. I felt her arm around my shoulder, but I was numb.

A thousand different scenarios raced through my brain. I could have pulled Aly away from Uhla'ar. I could have used the Loculus of Strength. Plugged up the rift before he got to it.

"It's not your fault . . ." Mom said, as if she were reading my mind.

I looked around. I knew this looked odd. I wasn't supposed to know Sister Nancy. Her putting her arm around
me was risky. But no one seemed to be noticing. Their eyes
were fixed toward the sea.

The once-narrow beach was now a vast expanse of sand,
littered with ancient driftwood planks and black clumps of
seaweed. It extended at least fifty yards to surf that was now
far away. Its waves crashed violently against the shore, but
at that distance it was barely audible. Beyond it, the black
sea formed mountains that undulated, slowly rising and
sinking. A small whale flopped helplessly, trying to return
to the sea.

At the edge of the receding surf, battered by the
waves, was the tilted frame of a barnacle-covered ship.
Its masts had broken off and its hull had mostly given
way to rot.

But the wood that remained was sturdy and thick, its
bow slathered with seaweed. Except for one section, where
the vegetation had been pulled away by the movement of
the rising land.

As I stared at it, I felt my entire body sink.

It's something much worse, Nirvana had said. Now I saw
what she meant.

It had started.

The continent was rising.

READ A SNEAK PEEK OF BOOK FIVE

THE LEGEND OF THE RIFT

FIRST DAY OF THE END OF THE WORLD

YOU KNOW YOU'VE reached rock bottom when you're standing on a beach, looking to the horizon, and you don't notice you're ankle-deep in dead fish.

If I'd been there ten minutes earlier, the water would be up to my shoulders. Now I was at the top of a wet, sloping plain. It was littered with rocks, ropes, bottles, crabs, fish, a massive but motionless shark, and the rotted hull of an old shipwreck.

Our tropical island had shot upward like an express elevator. Ten minutes ago, King Uhla'ar of Atlantis had opened a rift in time, which according to legend would make the great continent rise again. But I wasn't really thinking about legends right then. Because when he jumped into that rift, he took Aly Black with him. One minute there, the next minute *boom*! Down and gone. Back into time. Back to Atlantis.

Losing Aly was like losing a part of myself.

So on the first day of the end of the world, I, Jack McKinley, felt like someone had reached down my throat and torn out my heart.

"Jack! Marco! Cass! Eloise!"

Mom.

I spun around at her voice. She was back on the sandy part of the beach, glancing over her shoulder. Behind us, a group of frightened Massa soldiers streamed out of the jungle. Marco Ramsay, Cass Williams, and his sister, Eloise, were standing at either side of me. And that was when I began to notice the fish. Because a really ugly one whipped my left ankle with its fin.

"They look nasty," Eloise said.

"They speak highly of you," Cass replied.

Eloise looked at him, completely baffled. "Who, the Massa?"

"No, the fish," Cass said. "Aren't you talking about the—"

"I'm talking about *those* guys!" Eloise said, pointing to the frantic soldiers. "Do you hear Sister Nancy—I mean, Jack's mom? She's warning us to stay out of their way."

From deep in the trees, I could hear the shrill screech of a poison-spitting vizzeet—followed by the guttural cry of a soldier in great pain.